Little Miss Grouch

Samuel Hopkins Adams

Illustrated by R. M. Crosby

"GOOD-NIGHT, SHE SAID, "AND—THANK YOU"

Little Miss Grouch

A NARRATIVE BASED UPON THE
PRIVATE LOG OF
ALEXANDER FORSYTH SMITH'S
MAIDEN TRANSATLANTIC
VOYAGE

BY
SAMUEL HOPKINS ADAMS

With Illustrations by
R. M. Crosby

1914

Illustrations

I

First day out.
  Weather horrible, uncertain and squally, but interesting.
  Developments promised.
  Feel fine.

SMITH'S LOG.

Several tugs were persuasively nudging the Clan Macgregor out from her pier. Beside the towering flanks of the sea-monster, newest and biggest of her species, they seemed absurdly inadequate to the job. But they made up for their insignificance by self-important and fussy puffings and pipings, while, like an elephant harried by terriers, the vast mass slowly swung outward toward the open. From the pier there arose a composite clamor of farewell.

The Tyro gazed down upon this lively scene with a feeling of loneliness. No portion of the ceremonial of parting appertained personally to him. He had had his fair fraction in the form of a crowd of enthusiastic friends who came to see him off on his maiden voyage. They, however, retired early, acting as escort to his tearful mother and sister who had given way to uncontrollable grief early in the proceedings, on a theory held, I believe, by the generality of womankind in the face of considerable evidence to the contrary, that a first-time voyager seldom if ever comes back alive. Lacking individual attention, the Tyro decided to appropriate a share of the communal. Therefore he bowed and waved indiscriminately, and was distinctly cheered up by a point-blank smile and handkerchief flutter from a piquant brunette who liked his looks. Most people liked his looks, particularly women.

In the foreground of the dock was an individual who apparently didn't. He was a fashionable and frantic oldish-young man, who had burst through the barrier and now jigged upon the pier-head in a manner not countenanced by the Society for Standardizing Ballroom Dances. At intervals he made gestures toward the Tyro as if striving, against unfair odds of distance, to sweep him from the surface of creation. As the Tyro had never before set eyes upon him, this was surprising. The solution of the mystery came from the crowd, close-pressed about the Tyro. It took the form of an unmistakable sniffle, and it somehow contrived to be indubitably and rather pitifully feminine. The Tyro turned.

At, or rather underneath, his left shoulder, and trying to peep over or past it, he beheld a small portion of a most woe-begone little face, heavily swathed against the nipping March wind. Through the beclouding veil he could dimly make out that the eyes were swollen, the cheeks were mottled; even the nose—with regret I state it—was red and puffy. An unsightly, melancholy little spectacle to which the Tyro's young heart went out in prompt pity. It had a habit of going out in friendly and helpful wise to forlorn and unconsidered people, to the kind of folk that nobody else had time to bother about.

"What a mess of a face, poor kiddy!" said the Tyro to himself.

From the mess came another sniffle and then a gurgle. The Tyro, with a lithe movement of his body, slipped aside from his position of vantage, and the pressure of the crowd brought the girl against the rail. Thereupon the Seven Saltatory Devils possessing the frame of the frantic and fashionable dock-dancer deserted it, yielding place to a demon of vocality.

"I think he's calling to you," said the Tyro in the girl's ear.

The girl shook her head with a vehemence which imparted not so much denial as an "I-don't-care-if-he-is" impression.

Stridently sounded the voice of distress from the pier. "Pilot-boat," it yelled, and repeated it. "Pilot! Pilot! Come—back—pilot-boat."

Again the girl shook her head, this time so violently that her hair— soft, curly, luxuriant hair—loosened and clouded about her forehead and ears. In a voice no more than a husky, tremulous whisper, which was too low even to be intended to carry across the widening waterspace, and therefore manifestly purposed for the establishment of her own conviction, she said:

"I wo-won't. I *won't*. I WON'T!!!" At the third declaration she brought a saber-edged heel down square upon the most afflicted toe of a very sore foot which the Tyro had been nursing since a collision in the squash court some days previous. Involuntarily he uttered a cry of anguish, followed by a monosyllabic quotation from the original Anglo-Saxon. The girl turned upon him a baleful face, while the long-distance conversationalist on the dock reverted to his original possession and faded from sight in a series of involuted spasms.

"*What* did you say?" she demanded, still in that hushed and catchy voice.

"'Hell,'" repeated the Tyro, in a tone of explication, "'is paved with good intentions.' It's a proverb."

"I know that as well as you do," she whispered resentfully. "But what has that to do with—with me?"

"Lord! What a vicious little spitfire it is," said he to himself. Then, aloud: "It was my good intention to remove that foot and substitute the other one, which is better able to sustain—"

"Was that your foot I stepped on?"

"It *was*. It is now a picturesque and obsolete ruin."

"It had no right to be there."

"But that's where I've always kept it," he protested, "right at the end of that leg."

"If you want me to say I'm sorry, I won't, I *won't*—I—"

"Help!" cried the Tyro. "One more of those 'won'ts' and I'm a cripple for life."

There was a convulsive movement of the features beneath the heavy veil, which the Tyro took to be the beginning of a smile. He was encouraged. The two young people were practically alone now, the crowd having moved forward for sight of a French liner sweeping proudly up the river. The girl turned her gaze upon the injured member.

"Did I really hurt you much?" she asked, still whispering.

"Not a bit," lied the Tyro manfully. "I just made that an excuse to get you to talk."

"Indeed!" The head tilted up, furnishing to the Tyro the distinct moulding, under the blurring fabric, of a determined and resentful chin. "Well, I can't talk. I can only whisper."

"Sore throat?"

"No."

"Well, it's none of my business," conceded the Tyro. "But you rather looked as if—as if you were in trouble, and I thought perhaps I could help you."

"I don't want any help. I'm all right." To prove which she began to cry again.

The Tyro led her over to a deck-chair and made her sit down. "Of course you are. You just sit there and think how all-right you are for five minutes and then you *will* be all right."

"But I'm not going back. Never! Never!! *Nev-ver!!!*"

"Certainly not," said the Tyro soothingly.

4

"You speak to me as if I were a child!"

"So you are—almost."

"That's what they all think at home. That's why I'm—I'm running away from them," she wailed, in a fresh access of self-commiseration.

"Running away! To Europe?"

"Where did you think this ship was bound for?"

"But—all alone?" queried the other, thunderstruck.

"All alone?" She contrived to inform her whisper with a malicious mimicry of his dismay. "I suppose the girls you know take the whole family along when they run away. Idiot!"

"Go ahead!" he encouraged her. "Take it out on me. Relieve your feelings. You can't hurt mine."

"I haven't even got a maid with me," mourned the girl. "She got left. F-f-father will have a fu-fu-fit!"

"Father was practicing for it, according to my limited powers of observation, when last seen."

"What! Where did you see him?"

"Wasn't it father who was giving the commendable imitation of a whirling dervish on the pier-head?"

"Heavens, no! That's the—the man I'm running away from."

"The plot thickens. I thought it was your family you were eluding."

"Everybody! Everything! And I'm *never* coming back. There's no way they can get me now, is there?"

A reiterated word of the convulsive howler on the dock had stuck in the Tyro's mind. "What about the pilot-boat?"

"Oh! Could they? What shall I do? I *won't* go back. I'll jump overboard first. And you do nothing but stand there like a ninny."

"Many thanks, gentle maiden," returned her companion, unperturbed, "for this testimonial of confidence and esteem. With every inclination to aid and abet any crime or misdemeanor within reach, I nevertheless think I ought to be let in on the secret before I commit myself finally."

"It—it's that Thing on the dock."

"So you led me to infer."

"He wants to marry me."

"Well, America is the land of boundless ambitions," observed the young man politely.

"But they'll make me marry him if I stay," came the half-strangled whisper. "I'm engaged to him, I tell you."

"No; you didn't tell me anything of the sort. Why, he's old enough to be your father."

"Older!" she asseverated spitefully. "And hatefuller than he is old."

"Why do such a thing?"

"I didn't do it."

"Then he did it all himself? I thought it took two to make an engagement."

"It does. Father was the other one."

"Oh! Father is greatly impressed with our acrobatic friend's eligibility as son-in-law?"

"Well, of course, he's got plenty of money, and a splendid position, and all that. And I—I—I didn't exactly say 'No.' But when I saw it in the newspapers, all spread out for everybody to read—"

"Hello! It got into the papers, did it?"

"Yesterday morning. Father put it in; I *know* he did. I cried all night, and this morning I had Marie pack my things, and I made a rush for this old ship, and they didn't have anything for me but a stuffy little hole 'way down in the hold somewhere, and I wish I were dead!"

"Oh, cheer up!" counseled the Tyro. "I've got an awfully decent stateroom—123 D, and if you want to change—"

"Why, I'm 129 D. That's the same kind of room in the same passage. Do you call *that* fit to live in?"

Now the Tyro is a person of singularly equable temperament. But to have an offer which he had made only with self-sacrificing effort thus cavalierly received by a red-nosed, blear-eyed, impudent little chittermouse (thus, I must reluctantly admit, did he mentally characterize his new acquaintance), was just a bit too much.

"You don't have to accept the offer, you know," he assured her. "I only made it to be offensive. And as I've apparently been successful beyond my fondest hopes, I will now waft myself away."

There was some kind of struggle in which the lachrymose maiden's whole anatomy seemed involved, and then a gloved hand went out appealingly.

"Meaning that you're sorry?" inquired the Tyro sternly.

Some sounds there are which elude the efforts of the most onomatopœic pen. Still, as nearly as may be—

"Buh!" said the damsel. "Buh—huh—*huh!*"

"Oh, in that case." The Tyro turned back.

There was a long pause, while the girl struggled for self-command, during which her squire had time to observe with some surprise that she had a white glove on her left hand and a tan one on her right, and that her apparel seemed to have been put on without due regard to the cardinal points of the compass. Through the veil she perceived and interpreted his appraisal.

"I'm a dowdy frump!" she lamented, half-voiced. "I dressed myself while Marie was packing. But you needn't be so—so supercilious about it."

"I'm not," protested he, conscience-stricken.

"You are! When you look at me that way I hate you! I'm not sorry I was nasty to you. I'm glad! I wish I'd been nastier!"

The Tyro bent upon her a fascinated but baleful regard. "Angel child," said he in sugared accents, "appease my curiosity. Answer me one question."

"I won't. What is it?"

"Did you ever have your ears boxed?"

"Never!" she said indignantly.

"I thought as much."

"You'd like to do it, perhaps."

"I'd love to. It would do me—I mean you—so much good."

"Maybe I'll let you if you'll help me get away. I know they'll find me!" At the prospect the melancholy one once more abandoned herself to the tragedy of existence. "And you don't do a thing but m-m-make fu-fu-fun of me."

Contrition softened the heart of the Tyro. "Oh, look here, Niobe," he began.

"My name *isn't* Niobe!"

"Well, your nature's distinctly Niobish. I've got to call you something."

"You haven't! You haven't got to ever speak to me again. They'll find me, and catch me, and send me back, and I'll marry that—that *Creature*, if that's what you want."

This was the *argumentum ad hominem* with a vengeance. "*I* want? What on earth have I got to do with it?"

"Nothing! Nobody has anything to do with it. Nobody gives a—a—a *darn* for me. Oh, I wish I were back home!"

"Now you're talking sense. The pilot-boat is your play."

"Oh! And you said you'd help me." And then the last barrier gave way, and the floods swept down and immersed speech for the moment.

"Oh, come! Brace up, little girl." His voice was all kindness now. "If you're really bound to get away—"

"I am," came the muffled voice.

"But have you got any place to go?"

"Yes."

"Where?"

"My married sister's in London."

"Truly?"

"I can show you a cablegram if you don't believe me."

"That's all right, then. I'll take a chance. Now for one deep, dark, and deadly plot. If the pilot-boat is after you, they'll look up your name and cabin on the passenger list."

"I didn't give my real name."

"Oho! Well, your father might wire a description."

"It's just the kind of thing he would do."

"Therefore you'd better change your clothes."

"No. I'd better not. This awful mess is a regular disguise for me."

"And if you could contrive to stop crying—"

"I'm going to cry," said the young lady, with conviction, "all the way over."

"You'll be a cheerful little shipmate!"

"Don't you concern yourself about that," she retorted. "After the pilot leaves, you needn't have me on your mind at all."

"Thank you. Well, suppose you join me over in yonder secluded corner of the deck in about two hours. Is there anybody on board that knows you?"

"How do I know? There might be."

"Then stay out of the way, and keep muffled up as you are now. Your own mother wouldn't recognize you through that veil. In fact I don't suppose I'd know you myself, but for your voice."

"Oh, I don't always whisper. But if I try to talk out loud my throat gets funny and I want to c-c-cry—"

"Quit it! Stop. Brace up, now. We'll bluff the thing through somehow. Just leave it to me and don't worry."

"And now," queried the Tyro of himself, as he watched the forlorn little figure out of sight, "what have I let myself in for this time?"

With a view to gathering information about the functions, habits, and capacities of a pilot-boat, he started down to the office and was seized upon the companionway by a grizzled and sunbaked man of fifty who greeted him joyously.

"Sandy! Is it yourself? Well met to you!"

"Hello, Dr. Alderson," returned the young man with warmth. "Going over? What luck for me!"

"Why? Need a chaperon?"

"A cicerone, anyway. It's my first trip, and I don't know a soul aboard."

"Oh, you'll know plenty before we're over. A maiden voyager is a sort of pet aboard ship, particularly if he's an unattached youth. My first was thirty years ago. This is my twenty-seventh."

"You must know all about ships, then. Tell me about the pilot."

"What about him? He's usually a gay old salt who hasn't been out of sight of land for—"

"That isn't what I want to know. Does he take people back with him?"

"Hello! What's this? Don't want to back out already, do you?"

"No. It isn't I."

"Somebody want to go back? That's easily arranged."

"No. They don't want to go back. Not if they can help it. But could word be got to the pilot to take any one off?"

"Oh, yes. If it were sent in time. A telegram to Quarantine would get him, up to an hour or so after we cast off. What's the mystery, Sandy?"

"Tell you later. Thanks, ever so much."

"I'll have you put at my table," called the other after him, as he descended the broad companionway.

So the pilot-boat scheme was feasible, then. If the unknown weeper's father had prompt notice—from the disciple of Terpsichore, for example—he might get word to the pilot and institute a search. Meditating upon the appearance and behavior of the dock-dancer, the Tyro decided that he'd go to any lengths to see the thing through just for the pleasure of frustrating him.

"Though what on earth he wants to marry her for, *I* don't see," he thought. "She ought to marry an undertaker."

And he sat down to write his mother a pilot-boat letter, assuring her that he had thus far survived the perils of the deep and had already found a job as knight-errant to the homeliest and most lugubrious girl on the seven seas. At the warning call for the closing of the mails he hastened to the rendezvous on deck. She was there before him, still muffled up, still swollen of feature, and still, as he indignantly put it to himself, "blubbering."

Meantime there had reached the giant ship Clan Macgregor a message signed by a name of such power that the whole structure officially thrilled to it from top to bottom. The owner of the name demanded the instant return, intact and in good order, C.O.D., of a valuable daughter, preferably by pilot-boat, but, if necessary, by running the ship aground and sending said daughter ashore in a breeches-buoy, or by turning back and putting into dock again. In this assumption there was perhaps some hyperbole. But it was obvious from the stir of officialdom that the signer of the demand wanted his daughter very much and was accustomed to having his wants respectfully carried out. One feature of the message would have convinced the Tyro, had he seen it, of the fatuity of fatherhood. It described the fugitive as "very pretty."

The search was thorough, rigid, and quite unavailing. The reason why it was unavailing was this: At the moment when that portion of the chase to which the promenade deck was apportioned, consisting of the second officer, the purser, and two stewards, approached the secluded nook where the Tyro stood guardian above the feminine Fount of Tears, they beheld and heard only a young man admonishing a stricken girl in unmistakably fraternal terms:

"Now, Amy, you might just as well stop that sniveling. [The Tyro was taking a bit of revenge on the side.] You can't change your stateroom. There isn't another to be had on board. And if it's good enough for Mother, I think it ought to be good enough for you. Do have some gumption, Amy, and cut out the salty-tear business. Come on down and eat."

The pursuit passed on, and an hour later the pilot-boat chugged away passengerless; for even the mightiest cannot hold indefinitely an ocean liner setting out after a possible record. Almost at the moment that the man of power received a message stating positively that his daughter was not on the Clan Macgregor that perverse little person was saying to her preserver, who—foolish youth—had expected some expression of appreciation:—

"What do you mean by calling me Amy? I *hate* the name."

"Short for 'amiability,' your most obvious quality."

"You're a perfect *pig*!" retorted the lady with conviction.

The Tyro made her a low bow. "Oh, pattern of all the graces," said he, "I accept and appreciate the appellation. The pig is a praiseworthy character. The pig suffereth long and is kind. The pig is humble, pious, a home-lover and a home-stayer. You never heard of a pig changing his heart and running away across the seas on twelve hours' notice, because things didn't go exactly to suit him. Did you, now? The pig is mild of temper and restrained of speech. He always thinks twice before he grunts. To those that use him gently the pig is friendly and affectionate. Gratitude makes its home in that soft bosom. Well has the poet sung: —

"How rarer than a serpent's tooth
It is to find a thankless pig!

"The pig does not grouch nor snap nor stamp upon the feet of the defenseless. Finally and above all, he does not give way to useless tears and make red the lovely pinkness of his shapely nose. Proud am I to be dubbed the Perfect Pig."

"*Oh!*" said the tearful damsel, and potential murder informed the monosyllable.

"See here," said the Tyro persuasively: "tell me, why are you so cross with me?"

"Because you pitied me."

"Anybody would. You look so helpless and miserable."

"I'm not muh-muh-miserable!"

"I beg your pardon. Of course you're not. Any one could see that."

"I *am*. But I don't care. I *won't* be pitied. How dare you pity me! I hate people that—that go around pitying other people."

"I'll promise never to do it again. Only spare my life this time. Now I'm going to go away and stop bothering you. But if you find things getting too dull for you during the voyage, I'll be around somewhere within call. Good-bye, and good luck."

A little hand went out to him—impulsively.

"I *am* sorry," came the whisper—it was almost free of tragic effect this time—"and I really think you—you're rather a dear."

The Tyro marched away in the righteous consciousness of having done his full duty by helpless and unattractive girlhood. The girl retired presently to her cabin, and made a fair start on her announced policy of crying all the way from America to Europe. When, however, the ship met with a playful little cross-sea and began to bobble and weave and splash about in the manner of our top-heavy leviathans of travel, she was impelled to take thought of her inner self, and presently sought the fresh and open air of the deck lest a worse thing befall her. There in a sheltered angle she snuggled deep in her chair, and presently, braced by the vivifying air, was by way of almost enjoying herself. And thither fate drove the Tyro, with relentless purpose, into her clutches.

With his friend Alderson, who had retrieved him late in the afternoon after he had unpacked, the Tyro was making rather uncertain weather of it along the jerking deck, when an unusually abrupt buck-jump executed by the Macgregor sent him reeling up against the cabin rail at the angle behind which the girl sheltered.

"Let's stop here for a minute," panted Alderson. "Haven't got my sea-legs yet." There was a pause. "Did I see you making yourself agreeable to a young person of the dangerous sex a couple of hours ago?"

"Agreeable? Well, judging by results, no. I doubt if Chesterfield himself could have made himself agreeable to Little Miss Grouch."

"Miss *Who*?"

"Little Miss Grouch. Don't know her real name. But that's good enough for descriptive purposes. She's the crossest little patch that ever grew up without being properly spanked."

"Where did you run across her?"

"Oh, she wrecked my pet toe with a guillotine heel because I ventured to sympathize with her."

"Oh," commented the experienced Alderson. "Sympathy isn't in much demand when one is seasick."

"It wasn't seasickness. It was weeps for the vanished fatherland; such blubbery weeps! Poor little girl!" mused the Tyro. "She isn't much bigger than a minute, and *so* forlorn, and *so* red-nosed, and *so* homely, you couldn't help but—"

At this moment a drunken stagger on the part of the ship slewed the speaker halfway around. He found himself looking down upon a steamer-chair, wherein lay a bundle swathed in many rugs. From that bundle protruded a veiled face and the outline of a swollen nose, above which a pair of fixed eyes blazed, dimmed but malevolent, into his.

"Er—ah—oh," said the Tyro, moving hastily away. "If you'll excuse me I think I'll just step over the rail and speak to a fish I used to know."

"What's the matter?" inquired Alderson suspiciously, following him. "Not already!"

"Oh, no. Not that. Worse. That bundle almost under our feet when I spoke—that was Little Miss Grouch."

Alderson took a furtive glance. "She's all mummied up," he suggested; "maybe she didn't hear."

"Oh, yes, she did. Trust my luck for that. And I said she was homely. And she is. Oh, Lord, I wouldn't have hurt her poor little feelings for anything."

"Don't you be too sure about her being so homely. Any woman looks a fright when she's all bunged up from crying."

"What's the difference?" said the Tyro miserably. "A pretty girl don't like to be called homely any more than a homely one."

"There's where you're off, my son," returned Alderson. "She can summon her looking-glass as a witness in rebuttal."

"Anyway, I've put my foot in it up to the knee!"

"Oh, go up to-morrow when she's feeling better and tell her you were talking about the ship's cat."

"I'd show better sense by keeping out of her way altogether."

"You'll never be able to do that," said the sea-wise Alderson. "Try to avoid any one on shipboard and you'll bump into that particular person everywhere you go, from the engine-room to the forepeak. Ten to one she sits next to you at table."

"I'll have my seat changed," cried the other in panic. "I'll eat in my cabin. I'll fast for the week."

"You be a game sport and I'll help you out," promised his friend. "All hands to repel boarders! Here she comes!"

Little Miss Grouch bore down upon them with her much-maligned nose in the air. As she maneuvered to pass, the ship, which had reached the climax of its normal roll to port, paused, and then decided to go a couple of degrees farther; in consequence of which the young lady fled with a stifled cry of fury straight into the Tyro's waiting arms. Alderson, true to his promise, extracted her, set her on her way, and turned anxiously to his young friend.

"Did she bite you?" he inquired solicitously.

"No. You grabbed her just in time. This affair," he continued with profound and wretched conviction, "is going to be Fate with a capital F."

Meantime, in the seclusion of her cabin, the little lady was maturing the plot of deep and righteous wrath. "Wait till to-morrow," she muttered, hurling her apparel from her and diving into her bunk. "I'll show him," she added, giving the pillow a vicious poke. "He said I was homely! (Thump!) And red-nosed. (Plop!) And cross and ugly! (Whack!) And he called me Little Miss Grouch. And—and *gribble* him!" pursued the maligned one, employing the dreadful anathema of her schoolgirl days. "He pitied me. Pitied! Me! Just wait. I'll be seasick and have it over with! And I'll cry until I haven't got another tear left. And then I'll fix *him*. He's got nice, clear gray eyes, too," concluded the little ogress with tigerish satisfaction. "Ouch! where's the bell!"

For several hours Little Miss Grouch carried out her programme faithfully and at some pains. Then there came to her the fairy godmother, Sleep, who banished the goblins, Grief and Temper, and worked her own marvelous witchery upon the weary girl to such fair purpose that she awoke in the morning transformed beyond all human, and more particularly all masculine, believing. One look in her glass assured her that the unfailing charm had worked.

She girded up her hair and went forth upon the war-path of her sex.

II

Second day out.
  A good deal of weather of one kind and another.
  Might be called a what-next sort of day.
  I think I am going to like this old ocean pretty well.

SMITH'S LOG.

Where beauty is not, constancy is not. This perspicuous proverb from the Persian (which I made up myself for the occasion) is cited in mitigation of the Tyro's regrettable fickleness, he—to his shame be it chronicled—having practically forgotten the woe-begone damsel's very existence within eighteen short hours after his adventure in knight-errantry. Her tear-ravaged and untidy plainness had, in that brief time, been exorcised from memory by a more potent interest, that of Beauty on her imperial throne. Setting forth the facts in their due order, it befell in this wise:—

At or about one bell, to be quite nautical, the Tyro awoke from a somewhat agitated sleep.

"Hold on a minute!" protested he, addressing whatever Powers might be within hearing. "Stop the swing. I want to get out!"

He lifted his head and the wall leaned over and bumped it back upon the pillow. Incidentally it bumped him awake.

"Must be morning," he yawned. A pocket-knife and two keys rolled off the stand almost into the yawn. "Some weather," deduced the Tyro. "Now, if I'm ever going to be seasick I suppose this is the time to begin." He gave the matter one minute's fair and honorable consideration. "I think I'll be breakfasting," he decided, and dismissed it.

Having satisfied an admirable appetite in an extensive area of solitude, he weaved and wobbled up the broad stairs and emerged into the open, where he stood looking out upon a sea of flecked green and a sky of mottled gray. Alderson bore down upon him, triangulating the deck like a surveyor.

"Trying out my sea-legs," he explained. "How does this strike you as an anti-breakfast roll?"

"Hasn't struck me that way at all," said the Tyro. "I feel fine."

"Welcome to the Society of Seaworthy Salts! These are the times that try men's stomachs, if not their souls. Come along."

The pair marched back and forth past a row of sparsely inhabited deck-chairs, meeting in their promenade a sprinkling of the hardier spirits of the ship community.

"Have you seen Miss Melancholia this morning?" asked Alderson.

"No, thank Heaven! I didn't dare go in to breakfast till I'd peeked around the corner to make sure she wasn't there."

"Wait. She'll cross your bows early and often."

"Don't! You make me nervous. What a beast she must think me!"

"Here comes a girl now," said his friend maliciously. "Prepare to emulate the startled fawn."

The Tyro turned hastily. "Oh, that's all right," he said, reassured. "She's wholly surrounded by a masculine bodyguard. No fear of its being Little Miss Grouch."

A sudden roll of the ship opened up the phalanx, and there stood, poised, a Wondrous Vision; a spectacle of delight for gods and men, and particularly for the Tyro, who then and there forgot Little Miss Grouch, forgot Alderson, forgot his family, his home, his altars and his fires, and particularly his manners, and, staring until his eyes protruded, offered up an audible and fervent prayer to Neptune that the Clan Macgregor might break down in mid-ocean and not get to port for six months.

"Hello!" said Alderson. "Why this sudden passion for a life on the ocean wave?"

"Did you see her?"

"See whom? Oh!" he added, in enlightenment, as the escort surged past them. "That's it, is it, my impressionable young friend? Well, if you're planning to enter those lists you won't be without competition."

The Tyro closed his eyes to recall that flashing vision of youth and loveliness. He saw again the deliciously modeled face tinted to warmest pink, a figure blent of curves and gracious contours, a mouth of delicate mirth, and eyes, wide, eager, soft, and slanted quaintly at an angle to madden the heart of man.

"Is there such an angel as the Angel of Laughter?" asked the Tyro.

"Not in any hierarchy that I know," replied Alderson.

"Then there ought to be. Do you know her?"

"Who? The Angel of—"

"Don't guy me, Dr. Alderson. This is serious."

"Oh, these sudden seizures are seldom fatal."

"Do you know her?" persisted the Tyro.

"No."

The Tyro sighed. Meantime there progressed the ceremony of enthroning the queen in one of the most desirable chairs on the deck, while the bodyguard fussed eagerly about, tucking in rugs, handing out candy, flowers, and magazines, and generally making monkeys of itself. (I quote the Tyro's regrettable characterization of these acts of simple courtesy.)

"But I know some of her admirers," continued the other. "The lop-eared youth on the right is young Sperry, son of the famous millionaire philanthropist and tax-dodger, Diedrick Sperry. He'll be worth ten millions one of these days."

"Slug!" said the Tyro viciously.

"That huge youngster at her feet is Journay, guard on last year's Princeton team. He's another gilded youth."

"Unfledged cub," growled the Tyro.

"Very nice boy, on the contrary. The bristly-haired specimen who is ostentatiously making a sketch of her is Castleton Flaunt, the illustrator."

"*Poseur!*"

"The languid, brown man with the mustache is Lord Guenn, the polo-player."

"Cheap sport!"

"You don't seem favorably impressed with the lady's friends."

"Hang her friends! I want to know who she is."

"That also might be done. Do you see the tall man coming down the deck?"

"The old farmer with the wispy hair?"

"Precisely. That 'farmer' is the ablest honest lawyer in New York. Also, he knows everybody. Oh, Judge Enderby," he hailed.

"Howdy, Alderson," responded the iron-gray one. "Glad to see you. Now we shall have some whist."

"Good! Judge, do you know the pretty girl over yonder, in that chair?"

The judge put up an eyeglass. "Yes," he said.

"Tell my young friend here who she is, will you?"

"No."

"Why not?"

A cavernous chuckle issued from between the lawyer's rigid whiskers. "Because I like his looks."

"Well, I like hers, sir," said the Tyro naïvely.

"Very likely, young man. Very likely. So I'm helping to keep you out of trouble. That child is pretty enough to give even an old, dried-up heart like mine the faint echo of a stir. Think of the devastation to a young one like yours. Steer clear, young man! Steer clear!"

And the iron-gray one, himself an inveterate sentimentalist, passed on, chuckling over his time-worn device for quickening romance in the heart of the young by the judicious interposition of obstacles. He strolled over to the center of attraction, where he was warmly greeted. To the Wondrous Vision he said something which caused her to glance over at the Tyro. That anxious youth interpreted the look as embodying something of surprise, and—could it be?—a glint of mischief.

"Never mind," said Alderson, "I dare say we can find some way, some time to-day or to-morrow."

"To-morrow!" broke in the Tyro fretfully. "Do you realize that this voyage is only a five-day run?"

"Oh, Youth! Youth!" laughed the older man. "Are you often taken this way, Sandy?"

The Tyro turned upon him the candor of an appealing smile. "Never in my life before," he said. "I give you my word of honor."

"In that case," said his friend, with mock seriousness, "the life-saving expedition will try to get a rescue-line to the craft in distress."

With obvious hope the Tyro's frank eyes interrogated Judge Enderby as he returned from his interview.

"Still of the same mind, young man?"

"Yes, sir."

"Want to know her?"

"I do, indeed!"

"Very well. You have your wish."

"You're going to present me?"

"I? No, indeed."

"Then—"

"You say you wish to know her. Well, you do know her. At least, she says she knows you. Not all of us attain our heart's desire so simply."

"Know her!" cried the amazed Tyro. "I swear I don't. Why, I could no more forget that face—"

"Don't tell her that or she'll catch you up on it since she knows you have forgotten."

"What is her name?"

"Ah, that I'm forbidden to tell. 'If he has forgotten me so easily,' said she—and she seemed really hurt—'I think I can dispense with his further acquaintance.'"

"If I should break through that piffling bodyguard now —"

"If you want some rather high-priced advice for nothing," said the old and mischievous lawyer, "don't do it. You might not be well received."

"Are you in the secret, then?"

"Secret? Is there any secret? A very charming girl who says she knows you finds herself forgotten by you. And you've been maladroit enough to betray the fact. Naturally she is not pleased. Nothing very mysterious in that."

Thereupon the pestered youth retired in distress and dudgeon to his cabin to formulate a campaign.

Progress, however, seemed slow. It was a very discontented Tyro who, after luncheon, betook himself to the spray-soaked weather rail and strove to assuage his impatience by a thoughtful contemplation of the many leagues of ocean still remaining to be traversed. From this consideration he was roused by a clear, low-pitched, and extraordinarily silvery voice at his elbow.

"Aren't you going to speak to me?" it said.

The Tyro whirled. For a moment he thought that his heart had struck work permanently, so long did it remain inert in his throat. A sense of the decent formalities of the occasion impelled him to make a hasty catch at his cap. As he removed it, an impish windgust snatched it away from his nerveless grasp and presented it to a large and hungry billow, which straightway swallowed it and retired with a hiss of acknowledgment like a bowing Jap.

The Tyro paid not the slightest heed to his loss. With his eyes fixed firmly upon the bewitching face before him,—these apparitions vanish unless held under determined regard,—he cautiously reached around and pinched himself. The Vision interpreted his action, and signalized her appreciation of it by a sort of beatified chuckle.

"AREN'T YOU GOING TO SPEAK TO ME?"

"Oh, yes; you're awake," she assured him, "and I'm real."

"Wishes *do* come true," he said with the profoundest conviction.

Up went the Vision's quaintly slanted brows in dainty inquiry, with further disastrous results to the young man's cardiac mechanism.

"Have yours come true?"

"You have," he averred.

"Then you're glad to see me again?"

Again? *Again?* Here it behooved him to go cautiously. Inwardly he cursed the reticence of Judge Enderby with a fervor which would have caused that aged jurist the keenest delight. Then he made one more despairing call upon the reserve forces of memory. In vain. Still, he mustn't let her see that. Play up and trust to happy chance!

"Glad!" he repeated. "Don't you hear a sound of inner music? That's my heart singing the Doxology."

"Very pretty," the girl approved. "How is the poor foot?"

"Much better, thank you. Did you see that murderous assault?"

"See it? I?" The Vision opened wide eyes of astonishment.

"Yes. I didn't notice you in the crowd."

She gave him a long look of mock-pathetic reproach from under drooped lids. "Oh, false and faithless cavalier. You've forgotten me. Already!"

"Once seeing you, I couldn't forget you in ten thousand years," he cried. "There's some mistake. I don't know you."

Her laughter rippled about him like the play of sunlight made audible.

"Oh, antidote to vanity, look at me," she commanded.

"It's the very easiest task ever man was set to," he asserted with such earnestness that the color rose in her cheeks.

"Before I vanish forever, I'll give you your chance. Come! Who am I? One—two—thuh-ree-ee."

"Wait! You're Titania. You're an Undine of the Atlantic. You're the White Hope, becomingly tinged with pink, of American Womanhood. You're the Queen of Hearts and all the rest of the trumps in the deck. You are also Cleopatra, and, and—Helen of Troy. But above all, of course, to me you are the Sphinx."

"And you," she remarked, "are a Perfect Pig. 'The pig is a praiseworthy character. The pig suffereth—'"

"Little Miss Grouch!" The words burst from him with the propulsive energy of total amazement. The next instant he was submerged in shame.

"I never saw anyone's ears turn scarlet before," she observed, with delicate and malicious appreciation of the phenomenon.

"It's a symptom of the last decay of the mind. But are you really the—the runaway girl?"

"I really am, thanks to your help."

"But you look so totally different."

"Well," she reminded him. "You said you probably wouldn't recognize me when you saw me again."

"I don't wholly believe in you yet. How did you work the miracle?"

"Not a miracle at all. I just took the advice of a chance acquaintance and cheered up."

"Then please stay cheered up and keep this shape. I like it awfully."

"It's very hard to be cheerful when one is forgotten overnight," she complained.

"There's some excuse for me. You didn't have on this—this angel-cloth dress; and you looked so—"

"Dowdy," she put in promptly. "So you said—quite loud."

"Be merciful! I never did really get a good look at you, you know. Just the tip of your nose—"

"Red."

"Help! And a glimpse of your face through a mess of veils—"

"Such a mess of a face."

"Spare my life! How can I apologize properly when you—"

"You're beyond all apology. Couldn't you at least recognize my voice? I'm supposed, in spite of my facial defects, to have rather a pleasant voice."

"But, you see, you didn't do anything but whisper—"

"And blubber. It isn't a pretty word, but I have it on good authority."

"I'll commit suicide by any method you select."

She regarded thoughtfully her downcast victim, and found him good to look at. "So you prefer me in this form, do you?" she taunted.

"Infinitely. It couldn't be improved on. So if you've any more lightning changes up your sleeve, don't spring 'em. What does this particular manifestation of your personality call itself."

"Little Miss Grouch."

"Don't be vengeful."

"Niobe, then."

"That was the changeling."

"At any rate, it isn't Amy, short for amiability. To you I shall continue to be Little Miss Grouch until further notice."

"Is that my punishment?"

"Part of it."

"Well, I can stand it if you can," he declared recklessly. "What's the rest?"

"I think," she said, after deliberating with herself, "that I shall sentence you to slavery. You are to be at my beck and call until you've attained a proper pitch of repentance and are ready to admit that I'm not as hopelessly homely as you told your friend."

"Homely!" cried the harassed youth. "I think you're the most wond—hum!" He broke off, catching himself just in time. "You say this slavery business is to last until I make my recantation?" he inquired cunningly.

"At least."

He assumed a judicial pose. "Calls for consideration. Would you mind tilting the face a little to the left?"

"Gracious! Another artist? Mr. Flaunt has been plaguing me all the morning to sit to him."

"No, I'm not an artist. Simply a connoisseur. Now that I look more closely, your eyebrows are slanted a full degree too much to the north."

"My nurse was a Jap. Do you think Oriental influence could account for it?" she asked anxiously.

"And at the corner of your mouth there is a most reprehensible dimple. Dimples like that simply ought not to be allowed. As for your nose—"

"Never mind my nose," said she with dignity. "It minds its own business."

"No," he continued, with the air of one who sums up to a conclusion. "I cannot approve the *tout ensemble*. It's interesting. And peculiar. And suggestive. But too post-impressionistic."

"That is quite enough about me. Suppose you change the subject now and account for yourself."

"I? Oh, I came along to frustrate the plots of a wicked father."

"He isn't a wicked father! And I didn't ask you why you're here. I want to know who you are!"

"I'm the Perfect Pig."

Little Miss Grouch stamped her little French heel. As it landed the young man was six feet away, having retired with the graceful agility of a trained boxer.

"You're very light on your feet," said she.

"Therein lies my only hope of self-preservation. *You* were not very light on my foot yesterday, you know."

"Has it recovered enough to take me for a walk?"

"Quite!"

"Still," she added, ruminating, "ought I to go walking with a man whose very name I don't know?"

"My name? Do you think that's fair, when you won't tell me yours? Besides, I don't believe you'd care about it, anyway."

"Why shouldn't I?"

"Well, it isn't very impressive. People have even been known to jeer at it."

"You're ashamed of it?"

"No-o-o-o," said the Tyro artfully.

"You are! I'd be ashamed to be ashamed of my name—even if it were Smith."

"Hello! What's the matter with Smith?" demanded the young man, startled at this unexpected turn.

"Oh, nothing," said she loftily, "except that it's so awfully common. Why, there are thousands of Smiths!"

"Common? Well, I'll be jig—" At this point, resentment spurred the ingenuity of the Tyro to a prompt and lofty flight. "If you don't like Smith," he said, "I wonder what you'll think when you hear the awful truth."

"Try me."

"Very well," he sighed. "I suppose it's foolish to have any feeling about it. But perhaps you'd be sensitive, too, if you'd been born to the name of Daddleskink."

"What!"

"Daddleskink," said the Tyro firmly. "Sanders Daddleskink. Suppose you were Mrs. Sanders Daddleskink."

"I shan't suppose any such thing," she retorted indignantly.

"I warned you that you wouldn't like it."

"Like it? I don't even believe it. There ain't no such animile as a Daddleskink."

"Madame," said the Tyro, drawing himself up to his full height, "I would have you understand that, uneuphonious as the name may seem, the Daddleskinks sat in the seats of the mighty when our best-known American families of to-day, such as the Murphys, the Cohens, the Browns, Joneses, and Robinsons, were mere nebulous films of protoplasmic mud."

"Oo-ooh!" said Little Miss Grouch, making a little red rosebud of her mouth. "What magnificent language you use."

"Genealogists claim," continued the young man, warming to his subject, "that the family came from Provence and was originally De Dalesquinc, and that the name became corrupted into its present form. My friends often call me Smith for short," he concluded, in sudden inspiration.

"Very tactful of them," she murmured.

"Yes. You might have had the privilege, yourself, if you hadn't derided the name of Smith. Now, aren't you sorry?"

"I shall *not* call you Smith," declared the girl. "I shall call you by your own name, Mr. Sanders Daddle—Oh, it simply can't be true!" she wailed.

Chance sent Alderson along the deck at this moment. "Hello, Dr. Alderson," called the Tyro.

"Hello, Sandy!" said the other.

"You see," said the Tyro in dismal triumph.

Scant enough it was, as corroboration for so outrageous a facture as the cognomen Daddleskink, but it served to convince the doubter.

"At least, you have the satisfaction of being unusual," she consoled him.

"If you regard it as a satisfaction. Can you blame me for denouncing my fate? How will you like introducing such a name to your friends?"

"I'm not going to introduce you to my friends. I'm going to keep you for myself. Solitary confinement."

"Solitude à deux? That's a mitigation. Oh, beautiful—I mean to say plain but worthy *incognita,* suppose I ferret out the mystery of your identity for myself?"

"I put you on honor. You're to ask no questions of any one. You're not even to listen when anyone speaks to me. Do you promise?"

"May my eyes be blasted out and my hopes wrecked by never seeing you again, if I be not faithful," he said.

But Fate arranges these matters to suit its more subtle purposes.

The Wondrous Vision had dismissed her slave, giving him rendezvous for the next morning,—he had pleaded in vain for that evening,—and he was composing himself to a thoughtful promenade, and to the building of air-castles of which the other occupant was Little Miss Grouch, when he became aware of a prospective head-on collision. He side-stepped. The approaching individual did the same. He sheered off to port. The other followed. In desperation he made a plunge to starboard and was checked at the rail by the pursuer.

"I wish to speak to you," announced a cold and lofty voice.

The Tyro emerged from his glorious abstraction, to find himself confronted by a middle-aged lady with violent pretensions to youth, mainly artificial. Some practitioners of the toilet-table paint in the manner of Sargent; others follow the school of Cecilia Beaux; but this lady's color-scheme was unmistakably that of Turner in his most expansive mood of sunset, burning ships, and volcanic eruptions.

By way of compensation, she wore an air of curdled virtue, and carried her nose at such an angle that one expected to see her at any moment set the handle of her lorgnette on the tip thereof, and oblige the company with a few unparalleled feats of balancing.

Surprise held the Tyro's tongue in leash for the moment. Then he came to. Here was another unexpected lady evidently relying upon that tricky memory of his. Very well: this time it should not betray him!

"How do you do?" he said, seizing her hand and shaking it warmly. "I'm so glad to see you again."

She withdrew the captured member indignantly. "Again? Where have you ever seen me before?" she demanded.

"Just what I was trying to think," murmured the Tyro. "Where *have* I seen you?"

The colorful lady lifted her glasses and her nose at one and the same moment. "I am Mrs. Denyse," she informed him. "Mrs. Charlton Denyse. You may know the name."

"I may," admitted the Tyro, unfavorably impressed by the manner in which she was lorgnetting him, "but I don't at the moment recall it."

Exasperation flashed in Mrs. Denyse's cold eyes. She had spent much time and trouble and no small amount of money advertising that name socially in New York, and to find it unknown was a reflection upon the intelligence of her investment. "Where on earth do you come from, then?" she inquired acidly.

"Oh, all over the place," he answered with a vague gesture. "Mainly the West."

"So one would suppose. It doesn't matter. I wish you to read this." She thrust a folded newspaper page into his hand, adding: "It is only fair to you to say that I speak with the authority permissible to kinship."

SURPRISE HELD THE TYRO'S TONGUE IN LEASH

"Kinship? Do you mean that you're related to me?"

"Certainly not! Be good enough to look at the paper and you will understand."

The Tyro was good enough to look, but, he reflected with regret, he wasn't clever enough to understand.

The first column was given up to a particularly atrocious murder in Harlem. The second was mainly political conjecture. In the center of the page was a totally faceless "Portrait of Cecily Wayne, Spoiled Darling of New York and Newport, whose engagement to Remsen Van Dam has Just Been Announced." Beyond, there was a dispatch about the collapse of the newest airship, and, on the far border, an interview with the owner of the paper, in which he personally declared war on most of Central America and half of Europe because a bandit who had once worked on a ranch of his had been quite properly tried and hanged for several cold-blooded killings.

"You will gain nothing by delay," said the lady impatiently.

"I give it up," confessed the Tyro, returning the paper. "You'll have to tell me."

"Even the most impenetrable stupidity could not overlook the announcement of Remsen Van Dam's engagement."

"Oh, yes; I saw that. But as I don't know Mr. Van Dam personally, it didn't interest me."

"Still, possibly you're not so extremely Western as not to know who he is. He's the sole surviving representative of one of the oldest houses in New York."

"Barns, not houses," corrected the other gently. "His father was the Van Dam coachman. He made his pile in some sort of liniment, and helped himself to the Van Dam name when it died out."

For Mrs. Denyse to redden visibly was manifestly impossible. But her plump cheeks swelled. "How dare you rake up that wretched scandal!" she demanded.

"Scandal? Not at all," replied the Tyro mildly. "You see, I happen to know. My grandmother was a Miss Van Dam."

"It must have been of some other family," said the lady haughtily. "I beg to inform you that Remsen Van Dam is my cousin."

"Really! I'm awfully sorry. Still—you know,—I dare say he's all right. His father—the real name was Doody—was an excellent coachman. I've often heard Grandma Van say so."

Mrs. Denyse after a time recovered speech by a powerful effort, and her first use of it was to make some observations upon the jealousy of poor relations.

"But this is profitless," she said. "You will now appreciate the desirability of guarding your conduct."

"In what respect?"

Mrs. Denyse pointed majestically to the pictorial blur in the paper. "Perhaps you don't recognize that," she said.

"I don't. Nobody could."

"That's true; they couldn't," she granted reluctantly. "But there's the name beneath, Cecily Wayne. I suppose you can read."

"I can. Who is Cecily Wayne?"

"Of all the impudence!" cried the enraged lady. "As you've been making yourself and her conspicuous all the afternoon—"

"Oh!" exclaimed the Tyro, a great light breaking in upon him. "So that's Cecily Wayne. It's a pretty name."

"It's a name that half of the most eligible men in New York have tried their best to change," said the other with emphasis. "Remsen Van Dam is not the only one, I assure you."

"Then the apostle of St. Vitus on the dock was Remsen Van Dam! Well, that's all right. She isn't engaged to him. The paper's wrong."

"Pray, how can you know that?"

"A little bird—No; they don't have little birds at sea, do they? A well-informed fish told me."

"Then I tell you the opposite. Now I trust that you will appreciate that your attentions to Miss Wayne are offensive."

"They don't seem to have offended her."

"Where did you know her? Who are you, anyway?" snapped his inquisitress, her temper quite gone.

The Tyro leaned forward and fixed his gaze midway of the lady's adequate corsage.

"If you want to know," said he, "you're carrying my favor above your heart, or near it, this minute. Look on the under side of your necktie."

The indignant one turned the scarf and read with a baleful eye: "Smitholder: Pat. April 10, 1912." "What does Smitholder mean?" she demanded.

"A holder for neckwear, the merits of which modesty forbids me to descant upon, invented by its namesake, Smith."

"Ah," said she, with a great contempt. "Then your name, I infer, is Smith."

He bowed. "Smith's as good a trade name as any other."

"Very well, Mr. Smith. Take my advice and keep your distance from Miss Wayne. Otherwise—"

"Well, otherwise?" encouraged the Tyro as she paused.

"I shall send a wireless to my cousin. *And* to Mr. Wayne. I suppose you know, at least, who Hurry-up Wayne of Wall Street is."

"Never heard of him," said the Tyro cheerfully.

"You're a fool!" said Mrs. Charlton Denyse, and marched away, with the guerdon of Smith heaving above her outraged and ample bosom.

III

Third day out
   All kinds of doings, weather and otherwise.
   This is a queer old Atlantic.

SMITH'S LOG.

Overnight, Mrs. Charlton Denyse (wife of an erstwhile Charley Dennis who had made his pile in the wheat-pit) was a busy person. Scenting social prestige, of which she was avid, in connection with Cecily Wayne, she had sought to establish herself as the natural protectress of unchaperoned maidenhood and had met with a well-bred, well-timed, and well-placed snub.

Thick of skin, indeed, must they be who venture into the New York social scramble, and Mrs. Denyse shared at least one characteristic of the rhinoceros. Nothing daunted by her failure with the daughter, she proceeded to invest a part of the Dennis pile in wireless messages to Henry Clay Wayne, on the basis of her kinship with Remsen Van Dam. In the course of time these elicited replies. Mrs. Denyse was well satisfied. She was mingling in the affairs of the mighty.

She was also mingling in the affairs of the Tyro. To every one on board whom she knew—and she was expert in making or claiming acquaintance—she expanded upon the impudence of a young nobody named Smith who was making up to Cecily Wayne, doubtless with a hope of capturing her prospective millions. Among others, she approached Judge Enderby, and that dry old Machiavelli congratulated her upon her altruistic endeavors to keep the social strain of the ship pure and undefiled, promising his help. He it was who suggested her appealing to the captain.

As I have indicated, Judge Enderby in his unprofessional hours had an elfish and prank-some love of mischief.

Quite innocent of plots and stratagems formulating about him, the Tyro tried all the various devices made and provided for the killing of time on shipboard, but found none of them sufficiently lethal. At dinner he had caught a far glimpse of Little Miss Grouch seated at the captain's table between Lorf Guenn and the floppy-eared scion of the house of Sperry. Later in the evening he had passed her once and she had given him the most casual of nods. He went to bed with a very restless wonder as to what was going to happen in the morning, when she had promised to walk with him again.

Nothing happened in the morning. Nothing, that is, except an uncertain bobble of sea, overspread by a wind-driven mist which kept the wary under cover. The Tyro tramped endless miles at the side of the indefatigable Dr. Alderson; he patrolled the deck with a more anxious watchfulness than is expected even of the ship's lookout; he peered into nooks and corners; he studied the plan of the leviathan for possible refuges; he pervaded the structure like a lost dog. Useless. All useless. No Little Miss Grouch anywhere to be seen.

At noon he had given up hope and stood leaning against a stanchion in morose contemplation of a school of porpoises. They were very playful porpoises. They seemed to be actually enjoying themselves. That there should be joy anywhere in that gray and colorless world was, to the Tyro, a monstrous thing. Then he turned and beheld Little Miss Grouch.

She sat, muffled up in a steamer chair, just behind him. Only her eyes appeared, bright and big under the quaintly slanted brows; but that was enough. The Tyro was under the impression that the sun had come out.

"Hel-*lo*!" he cried. "How long have you been there?"

"One minute, exactly."

"Isn't it a glorious day?" said the Tyro, meaning every word of it.

"No; it isn't," she returned, with conviction. "I think this is a very queer-acting ship."

"No! Do you? Why, I supposed all ships acted this way."

"Well, they don't. I don't like it. I haven't been feeling a bit well."

The Tyro expressed commiseration and sympathy.

"*You* look disgustingly fit," she commented.

"I? Never felt so well in my life. A minute ago, I won't say. But now—I could burst into poetry."

"Do," she urged.

"All right, I will. Listen. It's a limerick. I made it up out of the fullness of my heart, and it's about myself but dedicated to you.

> "There once was a seaworthy child
> Whose feelings could never be riled.
> While the porpoises porped—"

"There's no such word as 'porped,'" she interrupted.

"Yes, there is. There has to be. Nothing else in the world acts like a porpoise; therefore there must be a word meaning to act like a porpoise; and that word is the verb 'to porp.'"

"You're an ingenious lunatic," she allowed.

"Dangerous only when interrupted. I will now resume my lyric:—

> "While the porpoises porped
> And the passengers torped—"

"The passengers *what*-ed?"

"Torped. What you've been doing this morning."

"I haven't!" she denied indignantly.

"Of course you have. You've been in a torpor, haven't you? Well, to be in a torpor, is to torp. Now I'm going to do it all over again, and if you interrupt this time, I'll *sing* it.

"There once was a seaworthy child
Whose feelings could never be riled.
　　While the porpoises porped
　　And the passengers torped,
He sat on the lee rail and smiled."

"Beautiful!" she applauded. "I feel much better already."

"Don't you think a little walk would put you completely on your feet?" he inquired.

"On yours, more probably." She smiled up at him. "Come and sit down and tell me: are you a poet, or a lunatic, or a haberdasher, or what kind of a—a Daddleskink are you?"

"Haberdasher? Why should I be a haberdasher?"

"An acquaintance of yours has been talking—trying to talk to me about you. She said you were."

"Mrs. Denyse?"

"She seems a fearfully queer person, and quite excited about you. There was something about you and a necktie, and—and Mr. Van Dam, and then I escaped."

"Oh! The necktie. Why, yes, I suppose I am a sort of haberdasher, come to think of it."

"I'm glad you're not ashamed of your business if you are of your name. You told her it was Smith."

"Did I? I don't remember that I did, exactly. Even so, what would be the use of wasting a really good name on her? She wouldn't appreciate it."

"Mr. De Dalesquinc—"

"Daddleskink," corrected the Tyro firmly.

"Very well," she sighed. "Daddleskink, then. Wasn't that Dr. Alderson, the historian, that you were walking with yesterday?"

"Yes. Do you know him?"

"Only by correspondence. He did some research work on my house."

"*Your* house. Do you inhabit a prehistoric ruin, that Alderson should take an interest in it?"

"I call it mine. It isn't really—yet. It doesn't belong to anybody."

"Then why not just go and grab it? Squatter sovereignty, I believe they call the process."

"I thought it was called jumping a claim. Somebody has a claim on it. But that doesn't count. I always get what I want."

"Without trying?"

"Yes," she purred.

"Unfortunate maiden!"

"What?"

"I said 'unfortunate maiden.' Life must be fearfully dull for you."

"It isn't dull at all. It's delightful!"

"As witness day before yesterday. Were you getting what you wanted then?"

"I wanted a good cry, and I got it. And I don't want to talk about it. If you're going to be stupid—"

"Tell me about the prehistoric ruin," he implored hastily.

"It isn't a ruin at all. It's the cunningest, quaintest, homiest little old house in all New York."

"I'm sorry," he said in the tone of one who reluctantly thwarts another's project.

"What are you sorry about?" She drew down the slanted brows with a delicious effect of surprise.

"I'm sorry; but you can't have that house."

"Why not?"

"It's mine."

"Now, you take any other house in New York that you want," she cajoled. "Fifth Avenue is still nice. Any one can live on Fifth Avenue, though. But to have a real house on Battery Place—that's different."

"My idea exactly."

She sat bolt upright. "You aren't serious. You don't mean the mosaic-front house with the little pillars?"

"The oldest house left on Battery Place. That's it."

"And you claim it's yours?"

"Practically. I don't exactly own it—"

"Then you never will. I've wished it in," she announced with the calmness of finality.

"Think how good for you it would be not to get something you wanted. The tonic effect of a life-size disappointment—"

"No," she said, shaking her head violently, "it wouldn't be good for me at all. I should cry and become a red-nosed mess again. *I'm—going—to—have—that—house.* Why, Mr. Dad—Mr. Smi—Mr. Man," she cried, with a gesture of desperation, "I've owned that house in my mind for five years."

"Five years! I've owned it for five generations."

"Are you claiming that it's your family place?"

"It is. Is it yours? Are you my long-lost cousin, by any chance? Welcome to my arms—coat of arms, I mean."

"What would that be?" she inquired mischievously, "a collar-button, fessed—"

"Bending above a tearful maiden rampant. The legend, 'Stand on your own feet; if you don't, somebody else will.'"

"I don't *think* I can boast any cousin named Daddleskink," she observed. "Anyway, we're not New Yorkers. We came from the West."

"Where the money is made," he commented.

"To the East where it is spent," she concluded.

"Why spend it buying other people's houses?"

"Daddleskink Manor," ruminated the girl, in mocking solemnity. "Shall you restore the ancient glory of the name? By the way, Dr. Alderson's researches don't seem to have brought your clan to light, in the records of the house."

"Oh, my interest is on my mother's side," said the Tyro hastily. "That's why I'm buying the property."

"You're not!" said the girl, with a little stamp of her foot. Her companion moved back apprehensively. "Can you pay a million dollars for it?"

"No. Can you?"

"Never mind. Dad said he'd get it for me if—if—well, he promised to, anyway."

"If you'd marry the marionette who recently faded from view?"

"Ye—yes."

"Far be it from me," said the Tyro modestly, "to enter the lists against so redoubtable a champion on such short notice. Still, if you *are* marrying real estate, rather than wealth, intellect, or beauty, I may mention that I've got an option on that very house, and that it will cost me pretty much every cent I've made since I left college to pay for it."

"That you've made? Haven't you got any money of your own?"

"Whose do you suppose the money I've made is?"

"But anything to *live* on, I mean. Do you have to work?"

"Oh, no. The poorhouse is contiguous and hospitable. But I've always had a puerile prejudice against pauperdom as a career."

"You know what I mean," she accused. "Haven't your people got money?"

"Enough. And they can use what they have. Why should they waste it on me?"

"But the men I know don't have to work," said the young lady.

There was nothing patronizing or superior in her tone, but the curiosity with which she regarded her companion was in itself an irritant.

"Oh, well," he said, "after you've bought an old historic house and maybe a coat of arms, I dare say you'll come to know some decent citizens by and by."

"You mustn't think I have any feeling about your working," she explained magnanimously. "Lots of nice men do. I know that. Only I don't happen to know them. Young men, I mean. Of course dad works, but that's different. I suppose Mrs. Denyse told you who dad is."

"She did. But I didn't know any more after she got through telling than before."

The slanted brows went up to a high pitch of incredulity. "Where in the world do you live?"

"Why, I've been in the West mostly for some years. My work has kept me there."

"Oh, your haberdashery isn't in New York?"

"My haber—er—well—no; that is, I don't depend on the—er—trade entirely. I'm a sort of a kind of a chemist, too."

"In a college?" inquired the young lady, whose impressions of chemistry as a pursuit were derived chiefly from her schooldays.

"Mainly in mining-camps. Far out of the world. That's why I don't know who you and your father are."

"Don't you really? Well, never mind us. Tell me more about your work," she besought, setting the feminine pitfall—half unconsciously—into which trapper and prey so often walk hand in hand.

He answered in the words duly made and provided for such occasions: "Not much to tell," and, as the natural sequence, proceeded to tell it, encouraged by her interested eyes, at no small length.

Little Miss Grouch was genuinely entertained. From the young men whom she knew she had heard sundry tales of the wild, untamed portions of our country, but these gilded ones had peeked into such places from the windows of transcontinental trains, or lingered briefly in them on private-car junkets, or used them as bases of supply for luxurious hunting-trips. Here was a youth—he looked hardly more—who had gone out in dead earnest and fought the far and dry West for a living, and, as nearly as she could make out from this gray-eyed Othello's modest narrative, had won his battle all along the line.

I am violating no confidence in stating that this was the beginning of trouble for Little Miss Grouch, though she was far from appreciating her danger at the time, or of realizing that her dire design of vengeance was becoming diluted with a very different sentiment.

"So," concluded the narrator, "here I am, a tenderfoot of the ocean, having marketed my ore-reducing process for a sufficient profit to give me a vacation, and also to permit of my buying a little old house on the Battery."

"I'm sorry," said Little Miss Grouch, imitatively.

"What are you sorry for?"

"Your disappointment. Still, disappointment is good for the soul. Anyway, I'm not going to quarrel with you now. You're too brutal. I think I'm feeling better. How do I look?"

"Like a perfect wond—hum!" broke off the Tyro, nearly choking over his sudden recollection of the terms of acquaintance. "I can't see any improvement."

"Perhaps walking would help. They say the plainest face looks better under the stimulus of exercise. Is your foot fit to walk on?"

"It's fit for me to walk on," said the Tyro cautiously.

"Come along, then," and she set out at a brisk, swinging stride which told its own tale of pulsing life and joyous energy. After half a dozen turns, she paused to lean over the rail which shuts off the carefully caged creatures of the steerage from the superior above.

"My grandfather came over steerage," she remarked casually. "I don't think I should like it."

A big-eyed baby, in its mother's sturdy arms below, caught sight of her and crowed with delight, stretching up its arms.

"Oh," she cried with a little intake of the breath, "look at that adorable baby!"

As she spoke the Tyro surprised in her face a change; a look of infinite wistfulness and tenderness, the yearning of the eternal mother that rises in every true woman when she gazes upon the child that might have been her own; and suddenly a great longing surged over his soul and mastered him for the moment. But the baby was lisping something in German.

"What is it saying?" Little Miss Grouch asked.

"OH, LOOK AT THAT ADORABLE BABY!"

"'Pretty-pretty,' substantially," translated the Tyro, recovering himself. "Madam," he continued, addressing the mother, "it is evident that your offspring suffers from some defect of vision. I advise you to consult an oculist at once."

"*Bitte?*" said the mother, a broad-shouldered, deep-chested young madonna.

"He says," explained Little Miss Grouch, "that it is a beautiful baby, with a wonderful intelligence and unusually keen eyes. What is her name?"

"Karl, lady," said the mother.

"Let's adopt Karl," said the corrected one, to the Tyro. "We'll come here every day, and bring him nougats and candied violets —"

"And some pâté de foie gras, and brandied peaches, and dry Martini cocktails," concluded the Tyro. "And then there'll be a burial at sea.

What do you think a baby's stomach is, beautiful—er—example of misplaced generosity? Oranges would be more to the purpose."

"Very well, oranges, then. And we'll come twice a day and meet our protégé here."

Thus it was arranged in the course of a talk with the mother. She was going back to the Fatherland, she explained, to exhibit her wonderful babe to its grandparents. And if the beautiful lady (here the Tyro shook his head vigorously) thought the captain wouldn't object, the youngster could be handed up over the rail for an occasional visit, and could be warranted to be wholly contented and peaceful. The experiment was tried at once, with such success that the Tyro was presently moved to complain of being wholly supplanted by the newcomer. Thereupon Little Miss Grouch condescended to resume the promenade.

"As our acquaintance bids fair to be of indefinite duration—" began the Tyro, when she cut in:—

"Why indefinite?"

"Since it is to last until I belie my better judgment and basely recant my opinion as to your looks."

"You were nearly caught while we were discussing our protégé. Well, go on."

"I think you'd best tell me a little about yourself."

"Oh, my life is dull compared with yours," she returned. "Our only interesting problem has been a barn-storming of the doors of New York Society."

"And did you break in?"

For a moment her eyes opened wide. Then she remembered his confessed ignorance and laughed.

With such reservations as she deemed advisable, she sketched briefly for him one of those amazing careers so typical of the swiftly changing social conditions of America.

As she talked, he visualized her father, keen, restless, resolute, a money-hunter, who had bred out of a few dollars many dollars, and out of many dollars an overwhelming fortune; her mother, a woman of clean, fine, shrewd, able New England stock (the Tyro, being of the old America, knew the name at once); and the daughter, born to moderate means, in the Middle West, raised luxuriously on the basis of waxing wealth, educated abroad and in America in a school which shields its pupils from every reality of life and forces their growth in a hothouse atmosphere specially adapted to these human orchids, and then presented as a finished product for the acceptance of the New York circle which, by virtue of much painful and expensive advertising in the newspapers, calls itself Society.

Part of this she told him, qualifying the grossness of the reality by her own shrewd humor; part he read between the lines of the autobiography.

What she did not reveal to him was that she was the most flattered and pampered heiress of the season; courted by the great and shining ones, fawned on by the lesser members of the charmed circle, the pet and plaything of the Sunday newspapers—and somewhat bored by it all.

The siege of society had been of farcical ease. Not her prospective millions nor her conquering loveliness, either of which might eventually have gained the entrée for her, would have sufficed to set her on the throne. Shrewd social critics ascribed her effortless success to what Lord Guenn called her "You-be-d——d" air.

The fact is, there was enough of her New England mother in Cecily to keep her chin up. She never fawned. She never truckled. She was direct and honest, and free from taint of snobbery, and a society perhaps the most restlessly, self-distrustfully snobbish in the world marveled and admired and accepted. Gay, high-spirited, kind in her somewhat thoughtless way, clever, independent of thought and standard, with a certain sweet and wistful vigor of personality, Cecily Wayne ruled, almost as soon as she entered; ruled—and was lonely.

For the Puritan in her demanded something more than her own circle gave her. And, true to the Puritan character, she wanted her price. That price was happiness. Hence she had fled from Remsen Van Dam.

"But what's become of your promenade deck court?" inquired the Tyro, when he found his attempts to elicit any further light upon her character or career ineffective.

"Scattered," she laughed. "I told them I wouldn't be up until after luncheon. Aren't you flattered?"

"I'm grateful," he said. "But don't forget that we have to call on Karl at four o'clock."

"Well, come and rescue me then from the 'court,' as you call it. Now I must make myself pretty—I mean less homely—for luncheon."

Leaden clogs held back the hands of the Tyro's watch after luncheon. Full half an hour before the appointed time he was on deck, a forehandedness which was like to have proved his undoing, for Judge Enderby, who had taken a fancy to the young man and was moreover amused by the incipient romance, swooped down upon him and inveigled him into a walk. Some five minutes before the hour, the Joyous Vision appeared, and made for her deck-throne attended by her entire court, including several new accessions.

Judge Enderby immediately tightened his coils around his captive. Brought up in a rigid school of courtesy toward his elders, the Tyro sought some inoffensive means of breaking away; but when the other hooked an arm into his, alleging the roll of the vessel,—though not in the least needing the support,—he all but gave up hope. For an interminable quarter of an hour the marplot jurist teased his captive. Then, with the air of one making a brilliant discovery, he said:—

"Why, there's your homely little friend."

"Who?" said the Tyro.

"Little Miss—what was it you called her?—oh, yes, Miss Grouch. Strange how these plain girls sometimes attract men, isn't it? Look at the circle around her. Suppose we join it."

The Tyro joyfully assented. The Queen welcomed Judge Enderby graciously, and ordered a chair vacated for him; young Mr. Sperry, whose chair it was, obeying with ill grace. The Tyro she allowed to stand, vouchsafing him only the most careless recognition. Was he not a good ten minutes late? And should the Empress of Hearts be kept waiting with impunity? Punishment, mild but sufficient for a lesson, was to be the portion of the offender. She gave him no opportunity to recall their appointment. And with a quiet suggestion she set young Sperry on his trail.

Now Mr. Diedrick Sperry, never notable for the most amiable of moods and manners, was nourishing in his rather dull brain a sense of injury, in that he had been ousted from his point of vantage. As an object of redress the Tyro struck him as eminently suitable. From Mrs. Denyse he had heard the story of the pushing young "haberdasher," and his suspicions identified the newcomer.

"Say, Miss Cecily," he said, "why 'n't you interdoose your friend to us?" In defense of the Sperry accent, I may adduce that, by virtue of his wealth and position he had felt at liberty to dispense with the lesser advantages of education and culture; therefore he talked the language of Broadway.

"What? To all of you?" she said lazily. "Oh, it would take much too long."

"Well, to me, anyway," insisted the rather thinly gilded youth. "I bin hearin' about him."

"Very well: Mr. Sperry, Mr. Daddleskink."

She pronounced the abominable syllables quite composedly. But upon Mr. Sperry they produced an immediate effect.

"Wha-at!" he cried with a broad grin. "What's the name?"

"Daddleskink," explained the Tyro mildly. "An umlaut over the K, and the final Z silent as in 'buzz.'"

"Daddleskink," repeated the other. "Daddle—Haw! haw! haw!!"

"Cut it, Diddy!" admonished young Journay, giving him a surreptitious dig in the ribs. "Your work is coarse."

Temporarily the trouble-seeker subsided, but presently above the conversation, which had again become general, his cackling voice was heard inquiring from Judge Enderby:—

"Say, Judge, how do you catch a diddleskink? Haw—haw—haw!"

This was rather further than the Empress intended that reprisals for *lèse-majesté* should go. Still, she was curious to see how her strange acquaintance would bear himself under the test. She watched him from the corner of an observant eye. Would he be disconcerted by the brusqueness of the attack? Would he lose his temper? Would he cheapen himself to answer in kind? What *would* he do or say?

Habituation to a rough, quick-action life had taught the Tyro to keep his wits, his temper, and his speech. No sign indicated that he had heard the offensive query. He stood quietly at ease, listening to some comments of Lord Guenn on the European situation. Judge Enderby, however, looked the questioner up and down with a disparaging regard and snorted briefly. Feeling himself successful thus far, Sperry turned from a flank to a direct onset.

"Know Mrs. Denyse, Mr. Gazink?" he asked.

"I've met her."

"How? When you were peddlin' neckties and suspenders?"

"No," said the Tyro quietly.

"Doin' much business abroad?" pursued the other.

"No; I'm not here on business. It's a pleasure trip," explained the victim pleasantly.

"Gents' furnishin's must be lookin' up. Go every year?" Mr. Sperry was looking for an opening.

"This is my first trip."

"Your first!" cried the other. "Why, I bin across fifteen times." He conceived the sought-for opening to be before him. "So you're out cuttin' a dash. A sort of haberdash, hey? Haw—haw—haw!" He burst into a paroxysm of self-applausive mirth over his joke, in which a couple of satellites near at hand joined. "Haw—haw—haw!" he roared, stimulated by their support.

The Tyro slowly turned a direct gaze upon his tormentor. "The Western variety of your species," he observed pensively, "pronounce that 'hee-haw' rather than 'haw-haw.'"

There was a counter-chuckle, with Judge Enderby leading. Mr. Sperry's mirth subsided. "Say, what's the chap mean?" he appealed to Journay.

"Oh, go eat a thistle," returned that disgusted youth. "He means you're an ass, and you are. Serves you right."

Sperry rose and hulked out of the circle. "I'll see you on deck— later," he muttered to the Tyro in passing.

Little Miss Grouch turned bright eyes upon him. "Mr. Daddleskink is not addicted to haberdashery exclusively. He also daddles in—"

"Real estate," put in the Tyro.

"Fancy his impudence!" She turned to Lord Guenn. "He wants to buy *my* house."

"Not the house on the Battery?" said one of the court.

"I say, you know," put in Lord Guenn. "I have a sort of an interest in that house. Had a great-grandfather that was taken in there when he was wounded in one of the colonial wars. The Revolution, I believe you call it."

"Then I suppose you will put in a claim, too, Bertie," said Miss Grouch, and the familiar friendliness of her address caused the Tyro a little unidentified and disconcerting pang.

"Boot's on the other leg," replied the young Englishman. "The house has a claim on us, for hospitality. We paid it in part to old Spencer Forsyth—he was my revered ancestor's friend—when he came over to England after the war. Got a portrait of him now at Guenn Oaks. Straight, lank, stern, level-eyed, shrewd-faced old boy—regular whackin' old Yankee type. I beg your pardon," he added hastily.

"What for?" asked the Tyro with bland but emphatic inquiry.

Lord Guenn was not precisely slug-witted.

"Stupid of me," he confessed heartily. "What should an American gentleman be but of Yankee type? You know,"—he regarded the Tyro thoughtfully,—"his portrait at Guenn Oaks looks a bit like you."

Little Miss Grouch shot a glance of swift interest and curiosity at the Tyro.

"Very likely," he said. "I'm a Yankee, too, and the type persists. Speaking of types, there's the finest young German infant in the steerage that ever took first prize in a baby-show."

As strategy this gained but half its object. Up rose Little Miss Grouch with the suggestion that they all make a pilgrimage to see the Incomparable Infant of her adoption. Much disgruntled, the Tyro brought up the rear. Judge Enderby drew him aside as they approached the steerage rail.

"Young man, are you a fighter?"

"Me? I'm the white-winged dove of peace."

"Then I think I'll warn young Sperry that if he molests you I'll see that—"

"Wait a moment, judge. Don't do that."

"Why not?"

"I don't like the notion. A man ought to be able to take care of himself."

"But he's twice your weight. And he's got a record for beating up waiters and cabbies about New York. Now, my boy," the judge slid a gaunt hand along the other's shoulder and paused. The hand also paused; then it gripped, slid along, gripped again.

"Where did you get those muscles?" he demanded.

"Oh, I've wrestled a bit—foot and horseback both," said the other, modestly omitting to mention that he had won the cowboy equine wrestling-match at Denver two years before.

"Hum! That'll be all right. But why did you tell those people your name was Daddleskink?"

"I didn't. Little Miss—Miss Wayne did."

"So she did. Mystery upon mystery. Well, I'm only the counsel in this case; but it isn't safe, you know, to conceal anything from your lawyer."

At this point the voice of royalty was heard demanding the Tyro. The baby, he was informed, wished to see him. If this were so, that Infant Extraordinary showed no evidence of it, being wholly engrossed with the fascinations of his new mother-by-adoption. However, the chance was afforded for the reigning lady to inform her slave that there was to be dancing that evening in the grand salon, and would he be present?

He would! By all his gods, hopes, and ambitions he would!

As he turned by his liege lady's side, an officer approached and accosted him.

"The captain would like to see you in his cabin at once, if you please."

*   *   *   *   *

Among those present at the evening's dance was *not* Alexander Forsyth Smith, *alias* Sanders Daddleskink. Great was the wrath of Little Miss Grouch.

IV

Fourth day out.
 I don't like this ship or anything
  about it; its laws, its customs,
  its manners, methods or morals.
I'm agin the government. Maritime
  law gives me a cramp. Me for the
  black flag with the skull and cross-bones.
As for this old Atlantic, I'd as
  soon be at the bottom as at the top —

SMITH'S LOG.

Peace reigned over that portion of the Atlantic occupied by the Clan Macgregor. The wind had died away in fitful puffs. The waves had subsided. Marked accessions to the deck population were in evidence. Everybody looked cheerful. But Achilles, which is to say the Tyro, sulked in his tent, otherwise Stateroom 123 D.

On deck, Little Miss Grouch sat, outwardly radiant of countenance but privately nursing her second grievance against her slave for that he had failed to obey her behest and appear at the previous evening's dance. Around her, in various attitudes of adoration, sat her court.

Mrs. Charlton Denyse tramped back and forth like a sentinel, watching, not too unobtrusively, the possibly future Mrs. Remsen Van Dam, for she expected developments. In the smoking-room Judge Enderby and Dr. Alderson indulged in bridge of a concentrated, reflective, and contentious species. As each practiced a different system, their views at the end of every rubber were the delight of their opponents. They had finished their final fiasco, and were standing at the door, exchanging mutual recriminations, when the Tyro with a face of deepest gloom bore down upon them.

"How much of the ship does the captain own, Dr. Alderson?" he asked, without any preliminaries.

"He doesn't own any of it."

"How much of it does he boss, then?"

"All of it."

"And everybody on board?"

"Yes."

"No one has any rights at all?"

"None that the captain can't overrule."

"Then he can put me in irons if he likes."

"Why, yes, if there be any such thing aboard, which I doubt. What on earth does he want to put you in irons for?"

"He doesn't. At least he didn't look as if he did. But he seems to think he has to, unless I obey orders. He threatened to have me shut up in my cabin."

"Hullo! And what have you been doing that you shouldn't do?"

"Talking to Little Miss Gr—Wayne."

"If that were a punishable offense," put in Judge Enderby, in his weighty voice, "half the men aboard would be in solitary confinement."

"I wish they were," said the Tyro fervently.

Judge Enderby chuckled. "Do you understand that the embargo is general?"

"Applies only to me, as far as I can make out."

"That's curious," said the archæologist. "What did you say to the captain?"

"Told him I'd think it over."

Judge Enderby laughed outright. "That must have occasioned him a mild degree of surprise," he observed.

"I didn't wait to see. I went away from that place before I lost my temper."

"A good rule," approved Dr. Alderson. "Still, I'm afraid he's got you. What do you think, Enderby?"

"I don't think non-professionally on legal matters."

"But what can the boy do?"

"Give me five dollars."

"What?" queried the Tyro.

"Give him five dollars," directed Alderson.

The Tyro extracted a bill from his modest roll and handed it over.

"Thank you," said the jurist. "That is my retainer. You have employed counsel."

"The best counsel in New York," added Dr. Alderson.

"The best counsel in New York," agreed the judge with unmoved solemnity; "in certain respects. Specializes in maritime and cardiac complications. You go out on deck and walk some air into Alderson's brain until I come back. He needs it. He doesn't know enough not to return a suit when his partner leads the nine."

"When one's partner is stupid enough to open a suit—" began the other; but the critic was gone. "So you've found out that Little Miss Grouch is Cecily Wayne, have you?" Alderson observed, turning to the Tyro.

"Whatever that may mean," assented the Tyro.

"It means a good deal. It means that she's Hurry-up Wayne's daughter for one thing."

"That also fails to ring any bell. You see, I've been so long out of the world. Besides, I don't want to be told about her. I'm under bonds."

"Very well. But the *paterfamilias* is a tough customer. I looked up some old records for him once, and was obliged to tell him a few plain facts in plainer English. He appeared to want me to give false expert testimony. To do him justice, he didn't resent my well-chosen remarks; only observed that he could doubtless hire other historians with different views."

"Was that about the Battery Place house?"

"Precisely. But how do you know—Oh, of course! You've got a sort of intangible interest in that, haven't you? Through your maternal grandmother."

"I've got more than that. I've got an option."

"Great Rameses! Are you the mysterious holder of the option?" Dr. Alderson laughed long and softly. "This is lovely! Does she know?"

"If she does, it hasn't shaken her confidence."

"Hire Enderby to unravel that," chuckled the other. "Here he comes back already. His interview must have been brief."

The lawyer approached, halted, set his back against the rail, and gazed grimly at the Tyro over his lowered spectacles. His client braced himself for the impending examination.

"Young man," the judge inquired, "what do you legally call yourself?"

"Smith. Alexander Forsyth Smith."

"What do you call yourself when you don't call yourself Smith?"

"Er—you heard! I've sometimes been called Daddleskink by those who don't know any better. That was only a little joke."

"It's a joke which Captain Herford seems to have taken to heart. He thinks you're a dangerous criminal traveling under the subtle *alias* of Smith."

"Can he lock me up for that?"

"Doubtless he can. But I don't think he will. Who's been sending back wireless messages about you?"

"Wireless? About me? Heaven knows; I don't."

"Could it have been Mrs. Charlton Denyse?"

"If they were uncomplimentary, it might. I'm afraid she doesn't approve of me."

"They seem to have been distinctly unfavorable. That Denyse female," continued the veteran lawyer, "is a raddled old polecat. Mischief is her specialty. How did she get on your trail?"

The Tyro explained.

"Hum! I'll bet a cigar with a gold belt around its stomach that the captain wishes she were out yonder playing with the porpoises. He doesn't look happy."

"What ails him?" inquired Dr. Alderson.

"Five different messages from Henry Clay Wayne, to begin with. Also, I fear my interview with him didn't have a sedative effect."

"What did you say to him?" asked his client.

"I informed him that I'd been retained by our young friend here, and that if he were restrained of his liberty without due cause we would promptly bring suit against the line. Thereupon he tried to bluff me. It's a melancholy thing, Alderson," sighed the tough old warrior of a thousand legal battles, "to look as easy and browbeatable as I do. It wastes a lot of my time—and other people's."

"Did it waste much of the captain's on this occasion?"

"No. He threatened to lock me up, too. I told him if he did, he and his company would have another batch of suits; a suit for every day in the week, like the youth that married the tailor's daughter.

"He called me some sort of sea-lawyer, and was quite excited until I calmed him with my card. When I left he was looking at my card as if it had just bitten him, and sending out a summons for the wireless operator that had all the timbre of an S.O.S. call. Young man, he'll want to see you about three o'clock this afternoon if I'm not mistaken."

"What shall I do about it?" asked the Tyro.

"Give me five dollars. Thank you. I never work for nothing. Against my principles. I'm now employed for the case. Go and see him, and keep a stiff upper lip. Now, Alderson, your theory that a man must indicate every high card in his hand before—"

Perceiving that he was no longer essential to the conversation the Tyro drifted away. Luncheon was a gloomy meal. It was with rather a feeling of relief that he answered the summons to the captain's room two hours thereafter.

"Mr. Daddlesmith," began that harried official.

"That isn't my name," said the Tyro firmly.

"Well, Mr. Daddleskink, or Smith, or whatever you choose to call yourself, I've had an interview with your lawyer."

"Yes? Judge Enderby?"

"Judge Enderby. He threatens to sue, if you are confined to your stateroom."

"That's our intention."

"I've no lawyer aboard, and I can't risk it. So I'll not lock you up. But I'll tell you what I can and will do. If you so much as address one word to Miss Wayne for the rest of this voyage, I'll lock *her* up and keep her locked up."

The Tyro went red and then white. "I don't believe you've got the power," he said.

"I have; and I'll use it. Her father gives me full authority. Make no mistake about the matter, Mr. Smith: one word to her, and down she goes. And I shall instruct every officer and steward to be on watch."

"As Judge Enderby has probably already told you what he thinks of your methods" (this was a random shot, but the marksman observed with satisfaction that the captain winced), "it would be superfluous for me to add anything."

"Superfluous and risky," retorted the commander.

The Tyro went out on deck because he felt that he needed air. Malign fate would have it that, as he stood at the rail, brooding over this unsurmountable complication, Little Miss Grouch should appear, radiant, glorious of hue, and attended by the galaxy of swains. She gave him the lightest of passing nods as she went by. He raised his cap gloomily.

"Your queer-named friend doesn't look happy," commented Lord Guenn at her elbow.

"Go and tell him I wish to speak with him," ordered the delectable tyrant.

The Englishman did so.

"I'm not feeling well," apologized the Tyro. "Please ask her to excuse me."

"You'd best ask her yourself," suggested the other. "I'm not much of a diplomat."

"No. I'm going below," said the wretched Tyro.

Well for him had he gone at once. But he lingered, and when he turned again he was frozen with horror to see her bearing down upon him with all sails set and colors flying.

"Why weren't you at the dance last night?" she demanded.

He looked at her with a piteous eye and shook his head.

"Not feeling fit?"

Another mute and miserable denial.

"I don't believe it! You aren't a bit pea-green. Quite red, on the contrary."

Silence from the victim.

"Besides, you know, you're the seaworthy child," she mocked.

> "'Whose feelings could never be riled.
>   While the porpoises porped
>   And the passengers torped,
> *He* sat on the lee rail and smiled.'

Here's the lee rail. Haven't you a single smile about you anywhere?"

He shook his head with infinite vigor.

"Can't you even speak? Is that the way a Perfect Pig should act?" she persisted, impishly determined to force him out of his extraordinary silence. "Have you made a vow? Or what?"

At that moment the Tyro caught sight of a gold-laced individual advancing upon them. With a stifled groan he turned his back full upon the Wondrous Vision, and at that moment would have been willing to reward handsomely any wave that would have reached up and snatched him into the bosom of the Atlantic.

Behind him he could hear a stifled little gasp, then a stamp of a foot (he shrank with involuntary memory), then retreating steps. In a conquering career Miss Cecily Wayne had never before been snubbed by any male creature. If her wishes could have been transformed into fact, the yearned-for wave might have been spared any trouble; a swifter and more withering death would have been the Tyro's immediate portion.

The officer passed, leveling a baleful eye, and the Tyro staggered to the passageway, and with lowered head plunged directly into the midst of Judge Enderby.

"Here!" grunted the victim. "Get out of my waistcoat. What's the matter with the boy?"

In his woe the Tyro explained everything.

"Tch—tch—tch," clucked the leader of the New York bar, like a troubled hen. "That's bad."

"Can he do it?" besought the Tyro. "Can he lock her up?"

"I'm afraid there's no doubt of it."

"Then what on earth shall I do?"

"Give me five—No; I forgot. I've had my fee."

"It's rather less than your customary one, I'm afraid," said the Tyro, with an effortful smile.

"Reckoned in thousands it would be about right. But this is different. This is serious. I've got to think about this. Meantime you keep away from that pink-and-white peril. Understand?"

"Yes, sir," said the Tyro miserably.

"But there's no reason why you shouldn't write a note if you think fit."

"So there isn't!" The Tyro brightened amazingly. "I'll do it now."

But that note was never delivered. For, coming on deck after writing it, its author met Little Miss Grouch face to face, and was the recipient of a cut so direct, so coldly smiling, so patent to all the ship-world, so indicative of permanent and hopeless unconsciousness of his existence, that he tore up the epistle and a playful porpoise rolled the fragments deep into the engulfing ocean. Perhaps it was just as well, for, as Judge Enderby remarked that night to his friend Dr. Alderson, while the two old hard-faced soft-hearts sat smoking their good-night cigar over the Tyro's troubles, in the course of a dissertation which would have vastly astonished his *confrères* of the metropolitan bar:—

"It's fortunate that the course of true love never does run smooth. If it did, marriages would have to be made chiefly in heaven. Mighty few of them would get themselves accomplished on earth. For love is, by nature, an obstacle race. Run on the flat, without any difficulties, it would lose its zest both for pursuer and pursued, and Judge Cupid would as well shut up court and become an advocate of race suicide. But as for that spade lead, Alderson—are you listening?"

"She's a devilishly pretty girl," grunted Dr. Alderson.

V

Fifth day out.
  A dull, dead, blank unprofitable calm.
  Nothing doing; nothing to do.
  Wish I'd gone steerage.

Smith's Log.

Legal employment is susceptible of almost indefinite expansion. Thus ruminated Judge Enderby, rising early with a brisk appetite for romance, as he fingered the two five-dollar bills received from his newest client.

For that client he was jovially minded to do his best. The young fellow had taken a strong hold upon his liking. Moreover, the judge was a confirmed romantic, though he would have resented being thus catalogued. He chose to consider his inner stirrings of sentimentalism in the present case as due to a fancy for minor diplomacies and delicate negotiations. One thing he was sure of: that he was enjoying himself unusually, and that the Tyro was like to get very good value for his fee.

To which end, shortly after breakfast he broke through the cordon surrounding Miss Cecily Wayne and bore her off for a promenade.

"But it's not alone for your *beaux yeux*," he explained to her. "I'm acting for a client."

"How exciting! But you're not going to browbeat me as you did poor papa when you had him on the stand?" said Miss Wayne, exploring the gnarled old face with soft eyes.

"Browbeat the court!" cried the legal light (who had frequently done that very thing). "You're the tribunal of highest jurisdiction in this case."

"Then I must look very solemn and judicial." Which she proceeded to do with such ravishing effect that three young men approaching from the opposite direction lost all control of their steering-gear and were precipitated into the scuppers by the slow tilt of a languid ground-swell.

"If you must, you must," allowed the judge, "though," he added with a glance at the struggling group, "it's rather dangerous. I'm approaching you," he continued, "on behalf of a client suddenly stricken dumb."

Miss Wayne's shapely nose elevated itself to a marked angle. "I don't think I want to hear about him," she observed coldly.

"He's in dire distress over his affliction."

"I have troubles of my own. I'm deaf."

"Then suppose I should express to you in the sign language that my client—"

"I don't want to hear it—see it—know anything about it." The amount of determination which Miss Wayne's chin contrived to express seemed quite incompatible with the adorable dimple nestling in the center thereof.

"Must I return the fee, then?"

"What fee?"

"The victim of this sudden misfortune has retained me—"

"To act as go-between?"

"Well, no; not precisely. But to represent him in all matters of import on this voyage. On two occasions he has paid over the sum of five dollars. I never work for nothing. Would you deprive a superannuated lawyer of the most promising chance to earn an honest penny which has presented itself in a year?"

"Poor old gentleman!" she laughed. "Far be it from me to ruin your prospects. But if Mr. Daddle—if your client," pursued the girl with heightened color, "has anything to say to me, he'd best say it himself."

"As I have already explained to the learned court, he can't. He's dumb."

"Why is he dumb?"

"Ah! What an ally is curiosity! My unhappy client is dumb by order."

"Whose order?"

"The captain's."

"Has the captain told him he mustn't speak?"

"To you."

All of Miss Wayne's dimples sprang to their places and stood at attention. "How lovely! What for? I'll make him."

"Ah! What an ally is opposition," sighed the astute old warrior. "But I fear you can't."

"Can't I! Wait and see."

"No. He is afraid."

"He doesn't look a victim of timidity."

"Not for himself. But unpleasant things will happen to a friend—well, let us say an acquaintance for whom he has no small regard—if he disobeys."

"Oh, dealer in mysteries, tell me more!"

"Thou art the woman."

"I? What can possibly happen to me?"

"Solitary confinement."

"I don't think that's a very funny joke," said she contemptuously.

"Indeed, it's no joke. Your eyes will grow dim, your appetite will wane, your complexion will suffer, that tolerable share of good looks which a casual Providence has bestowed upon you—"

"Please don't tease the court, Judge Enderby. What is it all about?"

"In words of one syllable: if the boy speaks to you once more, you're to be sentenced to your stateroom."

"How intolerable!" she flashed. "Who on this ship has the right—"

"Nobody. But on shore you possess a stern and rockbound father who, thanks to the malevolent mechanism of an evil genius named Marconi, has been able to exert his authority through the captain, acting *in loco parentis*, if I may venture to employ a tongue more familiar to this learned court than to myself."

"And that's the reason Mr. Daddleskink," she got it out, with a brave effort, "wouldn't speak to me yesterday?"

"The sole and only reason! Being a minor—"

"Gracious! Isn't he twenty-one?"

"If the court will graciously permit me to conclude my sentence — being a minor, you still — "

"I'm not a minor."

"You're not?"

"Certainly not. I was twenty-one last month."

"Your father gave the captain to understand that you were under age."

"Papa's memory sometimes plays tricks on him," said the maiden demurely.

"Or on others. I noticed that in the Mid & Mud Railroad investigation. You're sure you're over twenty-one?"

"Of course I'm sure."

"But can you prove it?"

"Gracious! How are such things proved? Is it necessary for me to prove it?"

"It would be helpful."

"What am I to do?"

"Give me five dollars," said the judge promptly.

"I haven't five dollars with me."

"Get it, then. I never work for nothing."

The ranging eye of Miss Wayne fell upon a figure in a steamer-chair, all huddled up behind a widespread newspaper. There was something suspiciously familiar about the figure. Miss Wayne bore down upon it. The paper—five days old—trembled. She peered over the top of it. Behind and below crouched the Tyro pretending to be asleep.

"Good-morning," said Miss Wayne.

A delicate but impressive snore answered her.

"Mr. Daddleskink!"

No answer. But the face of the victim twitched painfully. It is but human for the bravest martyr to wince under torture.

"Wake up! I know you're not asleep. I *will* be answered!" She stamped her small but emphatic foot on the deck. The legs of the Tyro curled up under as instinctively as those of an assailed spider.

"There! You see! You needn't pretend. Won't you please speak to me?" The tormentor was having a beautiful time with her revenge.

"Go away," said a hoarse whisper from behind the newspaper.

"I'm in trouble." The voice sounded very childlike in its plea. The Tyro writhed.

"Even if you don't like me"—the Tyro writhed some more—"and don't consider me fit to speak to"—the Tyro's contortions were fairly Laocoönish—"would you—couldn't you lend me five dollars?"

The Tyro blinked rapidly.

"I need it awfully," pursued the malicious maiden.

Desperation marked itself on his brow. He scrambled from his chair, plunged his hand into his pocket, extracted a bill, transferred it to her waiting fingers, and hustled for the nearest doorway. He didn't reach it. The august undulations of Mrs. Charlton Denyse's form intercepted him.

"This is shameless!" she declared.

For once the abused youth was almost ready to agree with her.

"COULDN'T YOU LEND ME FIVE DOLLARS?"

"What?" he said weakly.

"Don't quibble with me, sir. I saw, if I did not hear. You passed Miss Wayne a note. I am astonished!" she said, in the tone of a scandalized Sunday-School teacher.

The Tyro rapidly reflected that she would have been considerably more astonished could she have known the nature of the "note." From the tail of his eye he saw the recipient in close conversation with Judge Enderby. Remembering his own dealings with that eminent fee-hunter he drew a rapid conclusion.

"Would you like to know what was in that note?" he inquired.

"As a prospective connection of Miss Wayne's—"

"If so, ask Judge Enderby."

"Why should I ask Judge Enderby?"

"Because, unless I'm mistaken, he's got the note now."

"I shall not ask Judge Enderby. I shall report the whole disgraceful affair to the captain."

"Don't do that!" cried the Tyro in alarm.

"Perhaps that will put an end to your vulgar persecution of an inexperienced young girl."

"O Lord!" groaned the Tyro, setting out in pursuit of the lawyer as the protector of social sanctities turned away. "Now I *have* done it!"

He caught up with the judge and his companion at the turn of the deck. "May I have a word with you, Judge?" he cried.

"I'm busy," said the lawyer gruffly. "I'm engaged in an important consultation."

"But this can't wait," cried the unfortunate.

"Anything can wait," said the old man. "But youth," he added in an undertone.

"You've got to listen!" The Tyro planted himself, a very solid, set bulk of athletic young manhood, in the jurist's path.

"In the face of force and coercion," sighed the other.

"I've been seen speaking to Miss—Miss—"

"Grouch," supplied the indicated damsel sweetly.

"Mrs. Denyse saw us. She has gone to report to the captain."

Little Miss Grouch

"Lovely!" said the lawyer. "Beautiful! Enter the Wicked Godmother. The fairy-tale is working out absolutely according to Grimm."

"But Miss—"

"Grouch," chirped the young lady melodiously.

"—will be locked up—"

"In the donjon-keep," chuckled the lawyer. "Chapter the seventh. Who says that romance has died out of the world?"

"But if Mrs. Denyse carries out her threat and tells the captain—"

"The Wicked Ogre, you mean. If you love me, the Wicked Ogre. And he will lock the Lovely Princess in the donjon-keep until the dumb but devoted Prince arrives in time—just in the nick of time—to effect a rescue. That comes in the last chapter. And then, of course, they were mar—"

"I'm tired of fairy-tales," said Little Miss Grouch hastily. "It won't be a bit funny to be locked up—"

"With three grains of corn per day and a cup of sour wine. Hans Christian Andersen never did anything like this!" crowed the enchanted lawyer.

"Meantime," observed the Tyro, with the calm of despair, "Mrs. Denyse has found the captain."

"Presto, change!" said Judge Enderby, catching each by an arm and hurtling them around the curve of the cabin. "We come back to the dull reality of facts, retainers and advice. Fairy Prince,—young man, I mean,—you go and watch for icebergs over the port bow until sent for. Miss Wayne, you come with me to a secluded spot where the captain can't discover us for an hour or so. I have a deep suspicion that he isn't really in any great haste to find you."

As soon as they were seated in the refuge which the old gentleman found, he turned upon her.

"What are you trying to do to that young man?"

"Nothing," said she with slanted eyes.

"Don't look at me that way. It's a waste of good material. Remember, he's my client and I'm bound to protect his interests. Are you trying to drive him mad?"

Little Miss Grouch's wrongs swept over her memory. "He said I was homely. And red-nosed. And had a voice like a sick crow. And he called me Little Miss Grouch. I'm getting even," she announced with delicate satisfaction.

The old man cackled with glee. "Blind as well as dumb! There's a little godling who is also blind and—well, you know the proverb: 'When the blind lead the blind, both shall fall in the ditch.' Look well to your footsteps, O Princess."

"Is that legal advice?"

"Oh, that reminds me! You don't chance to have any documentary proof of your birth, do you?"

"With me? Gracious, no! People don't travel with the family Bible, do they?"

"They ought to, in melodrama. And this is certainly some ten-twenty-thirty show! Wise people occasionally have passports."

"Nobody ever accused me of wisdom. Besides, I left in a hurry."

"To escape the false prince. More fairy-tale."

"But I *am* twenty-one and I've got the very watch that papa gave me on my birthday."

"Let me see it."

She drew out a beautiful little diamond-studded chronometer of foreign and very expensive make.

"Most inappropriate for a child of your age," commented the other severely. "Ha! Here we are. Fairy Godfather—that's me—to the rescue." He read from the inner case of the watch. "'To my darling Cecily on her 21st birthday, from Father.' Not strictly legal, but good enough," he observed. "We shall now go forth and kill the dragon. That is to say, tell the captain the time of day."

"What fun! But—Judge Enderby."

"Well?"

"Don't tell Mr.—your other client, will you?"

"Why not?"

"I don't want him to know."

"But, you see, my duty to him as his legal adviser certainly demands that—"

"You're *my* legal adviser, too. Isn't my five dollars as good as his? Particularly when it really is his five dollars?"

"Allowed."

"Well, then, my age is a confidential communication and—what do you call it?—privileged."

"Oh, wise young judge! But, fair Portia, don't let me perish of curiosity. Why?"

"My revenge isn't complete yet."

"Look out for the inner edge of that tool," he warned.

With the timepiece in his hand, Judge Enderby bearded the autocrat of the Clan Macgregor on his own deck to such good purpose that Miss Cecily Wayne presently learned of the end of her troubles so far as prospective incarceration went. The knowledge, preserved intact for her own uses, put in her hand a dire weapon for the discomfiture of the Tyro.

Thereafter the ship's company was treated to the shameful spectacle of a young man hunted, harried, and beset by a Diana of the decks; chevied out of comfortable chairs, flushed from odd nooks and corners, baited openly in saloon and reading-room, trailed as with the wile of the serpent along devious passageways and through crowded assemblages, hare to her hound, up and down, high and low, until he became a byword among his companions for the stricken eye of eternal watchfulness. Sometimes the persecutress stalked him, unarmed; anon she threatened with a five-dollar bill. Now she trailed in a deadly silence; again, when there were few to hear, she bayed softly upon the spoor, and ever in her eyes gleamed the wild light and wild laughter of the chase.

Once she penned him. He had ensconced himself in a corner behind one of the lifeboats, where, with uncanny instinct, she spied him. Before he could escape, she had shut off egress.

"How do you do?" she said demurely.

He took off his cap, but with a sidelong eye seemed to be measuring the jump to the deck below.

"You've forgotten me, I'm afraid. I'm Little Miss Grouch. Would this help you to remember?"

She extended a five-dollar bill. He took it with the expression of one to whom a nice, shiny blade has just been handed for purposes of hara-kiri.

"I have missed you," she pursued with diabolical plaintiveness. "Our child—our adopted child," she corrected, the pink running up under her skin, "has been crying for you."

"Go away!" said the Tyro hoarsely.

"Are these the manners of a Perfect Pig?" she reproached him. And with adorable sauciness she warbled a nursery ditty:—

> "Lady once loved a pig.
> 'Honey,' said she,
> 'Pig, will you marry me?'
> 'Wrrumph!' said he.

"I can't grunt very nicely," she admitted. "*You* do it."

"Go away," he implored, gazing from side to side like a trapped animal. "Somebody'll see you. They'll lock you up."

"Me? Why?" Her eyes opened wide in the loveliness of feigned surprise. "Much more likely you. I doubt whether you really should be at large. Such a queer-acting person!"

"I—I'll write and explain," he said desperately.

"If you do, I'll show the letter to the captain."

He regarded her with a stricken gaze. "Wh—why the captain?"

"Being a helpless and unchaperoned young lady," she explained primly, "he is my natural guardian and protector. I think I see him coming now."

Legend is enriched by the picturesque fates of those who have historically affronted Heaven with prevarications no more flagrant than this. But did punishment, then, descend upon the fair, false, and frail perpetrator of this particular taradiddle? Not at all. The Tyro was the sole sufferer. Had the word been a bullet he could scarcely have dropped more swiftly. When next he appeared to the enraptured gaze of the heckler, he was emerging, *ventre à terre*, from beneath the far end of the life-boat.

"I'll be in my deck-chair between eight and nine to receive explanations and apologies," was her Parthian shot, as he rose and fled.

At the time named, the Tyro took particularly good care to be at the extreme other side of the deck, where he maintained a wary lookout. Not twice should the huntress catch him napping. But he reckoned without her emissaries. Lord Guenn presently sauntered up, paused, and surveyed the quarry with a twinkling eye.

"I'm commanded to bring you in, dead or alive," he said.

"It will be dead, then," said the Tyro.

"What's the little game? Some of your American rag-josh, I believe you call it?"

"Something of that nature," admitted the other.

"This will be a blow to Cissy," observed his lordship. "She's used to having 'em come to heel at the first whistle. I say, Mr. Daddleskink—"

"My name's not Daddleskink," the Tyro informed him morosely.

"I beg your pardon if I mispronounced it. How—"

"Smith," said the proprietor of that popular cognomen.

"I say," cried the Briton in vast surprise, "that's worse than our pronouncing 'Castelreagh' 'Derby' for short!"

"S-m-i-t-h, Smith. The other was a joke and a very bum one! Alexander Forsyth Smith from now on."

"Hullo! What price the Forsyth?" Lord Guenn regarded him with increased interest. "Did Miss Wayne say something about your having an interest in her house on the Battery?"

"My house," corrected the other. "Yes, I've got an old option, depending on a ground-lease, that's come down in the family."

"What family?"

"The Forsyths. My grandmother was born in that house."

"Then our portrait of the Yank—of the American who looks like you at Guenn Oaks is your great-grandfather."

"I suppose so."

"Well met!" said Lord Guenn. "There are some sketches of the Forsyth place as it used to be at Guenn Oaks that would interest you. My ancestor was a bit of a dab with his brush."

"Indeed they'd interest me," returned the Tyro, "if they show the old boundary-lines. My claim on which I hope to buy in the property rests on the original lot, and that's in question now. There are some other people trying to hold me off—But that's another matter," he concluded hastily, as he recalled who his rival was.

"Quite the same matter. It's Cecily Wayne, isn't it?"

"Her father, I suppose. And as far as any evidence in your possession goes, of course I couldn't expect—considering that Miss Wayne's interests are involved—"

"Why on earth not, my dear fellow?"

"Well, I suppose—that is—I thought perhaps you—" floundered the Tyro, reddening.

Lord Guenn laughed outright. "You thought I was in the universal hunt? No, indeed! You see, I married Cecily's cousin. As for the house, I'm with you. I believe in keeping those things in the family. I say, where are you going when we land?"

"London, I suppose."

"Why not run up to Guenn Oaks for a week and see your great-grandad? Lady Guenn would be delighted. Cissy will be there, I shouldn't wonder."

"That's mighty good of you," said the Tyro. A sudden thought amused him. "Won't your ancestors turn over in their graves at having a haberdasher at Guenn Oaks?"

"They would rise up to welcome any of the blood of Spencer Forsyth," said the Briton seriously. "But what a people you are!" he continued. "Now an English haberdasher may be a very admirable person, but—"

"Hold on a moment. I'm not really a haberdasher. While I was in college I invented an easy-slipping tie. A friend patented it and I still draw an income from it. It's just another of the tangle of mistakes I've gotten into. As people have got the other notion, I don't care to correct it."

"That rotter, Sperry," said Lord Guenn with a grin—"I was glad to see you bowl him over. He's just a bit too impressed with his money. Fished all over the shop for an invitation to Guenn Oaks, and when he couldn't get it, wanted to buy the place. Bounder! Then you'll come?"

"Yes. I'll be delighted to."

"Jove! I'm forgetting my mission. Are you going to obey the imperial summons?"

"Can't possibly," said the Tyro, "I'm very ill. Tell her, will you?"

Lord Guenn nodded. "Perhaps one of you will condescend to let me in presently on all these plots and counterplots," he remarked as he walked away.

Left to himself the Tyro floated away on cloudy imaginings of gold and rose-color. A week—a whole week—with Little Miss Grouch; a week of freedom on good, solid land, beyond the tyranny of captains, the espionage of self-appointed chaperons, and the interference of countless surrounding ninnies; a week on every day of which he could watch the play of light and color in the face which had not been absent from his thoughts one minute since—

Thump! It was as if a huge fist had thrust up out of the ocean's depths and jolted the Clan Macgregor in the ribs. Several minor impacts jarred beneath his feet. Then the engines stopped, and the great hulk began to swing slowly to starboard in the still water.

Excited talk broke out. Questions to which nobody made reply filled the air. An officer hurried past.

"No. No damage done," he cried back mechanically over his shoulder.

Presently the engine resumed work. The rhythm appeared to the Tyro to drag. Dr. Alderson came along.

"Nothing at all," he said with the *sang-froid* of the experienced traveler. "Some little hitch in the machinery."

"Do you notice that there's a slant to the deck?" asked the Tyro in a low voice.

"Yes. Keep it to yourself. Most people won't notice it." And he walked on, stopping to chat with an acquaintance here and there, and doing his unofficial part to diffuse confidence.

One idea seized and possessed the Tyro. If that gently tilted deck meant danger, his place was on the farther side of the ship. Quite casually, to avoid any suggestion of haste, he wandered around.

Little Miss Grouch was sitting in her chair, alone and quiet. As the Tyro slipped, soft-footed, into the shelter of a shadow, he saw her stretch her hand out to a box of candy. She selected a round sweet, and dropped it on the deck. It rolled slowly into the scuppers. Again she tried the experiment, with the same result. She started to get up, changed her mind and settled back to wait.

The Tyro, leaning against the cabin, also waited. With no apparent cause—for he was sure he had made no noise—she turned her head and looked into the sheltering shadow. She smiled, a very small but very contented smile.

An officer came along the deck.

"The port screw," he paused to tell the waiting girl, "struck a bit of wreckage and broke a blade. Absolutely no danger. We will be delayed a little getting to port, that's all. I am glad you had the nerve to sit quiet," he added.

"I didn't know what else to do," she said.

She rose and gathered her belongings to her. Going to the entrance she passed so near that he could have touched her. Yet she gave no sign of knowledge that he was there; he was ready to believe that he had been mistaken in thinking that her regard had penetrated his retreat. In the doorway she turned.

"Good-night," she said, in a voice that thrilled in his pulses. "And—thank you."

VI

Sixth day out.
  Bump! And we're three days late.
  Suits me. I don't care if we never get in.

Smith's Log.

Whoso will, may read in the Hydrographic Office records, the fate of the steamship Sarah Calkins. Old was Sarah; weather-scarred, wave-battered, suffering from all the internal disorders to which machinery is prone; tipsy of gait, defiant of her own helm, a very hag of the high seas.

Few mourned when she went down in Latitude 43° 10' North, Longitude 20° 12' West—few indeed, except for the maritime insurance companies. They lamented and with cause, for the Sarah Calkins was loaded with large quantities of rock, crated in such a manner as to appear valuable, and to induce innocent agents to insure them as pianos, furniture, and sundry merchandise. Such is the guile of them that go down to the sea in ships.

For the first time in her disreputable career, the Sarah Calkins obeyed orders, and went to the bottom opportunely in sight of a Danish tramp which took off her unalarmed captain and crew. Let us leave her to her deep-sea rest.

The evil that ships do lives after them, and the good is not always interred with their bones. For the better or worse of Little Miss Grouch and the Tyro, the Sarah Calkins, of whom neither of them had ever heard, left her incidental wreckage strewn over several leagues of Atlantic. One bit of it became involved with the Clan Macgregor's screw, to what effect has already been indicated. Hours later a larger mass came along, under the impulsion of half a gale, and punched a hole through the leviathan's port side as if it were but paper, just far enough above the water-line so that every alternate wave could make an easy entry.

The Tyro came up out of deep slumber with a plunge. He heard cries from without, and a strongly bawled order. Above him there was a scurry of feet. The engines stopped. Three bells struck just as if nothing had happened. He opened his door and the coldest water he had ever felt on his skin closed about his feet. The passageway was awash.

Jumping into enough clothing to escape the rigor of the law, the Tyro ran across to 129 D and knocked on the door. It opened. Little Miss Grouch stood there. Her eyes were sweet with sleep. A long, soft, fluffy white coat fell to her little bare feet. Her hair, half-loosed, clustered warmly close to the flushed warmth of her face. The Tyro stood, stricken for the moment into silence and forgetfulness by the power of her beauty.

"What is it?" she asked softly.

He found speech. "Something has happened to the ship."

"I knew you'd come," she said with quiet confidence.

"Aren't you afraid?"

"I *was* afraid."

A roll of the ship brought the chill water up about her feet. She shivered and winced. Stooping he caught her under the knees, and lifted her to his arms. Feeling the easy buoyancy of his strength beneath her, she lapsed against his shoulder, wholly trustful, wholly content. Through the passage he splashed, around the turn, and up the broad companionway. Not until he had found a chair in the near corner of the lower saloon did he set her down. Released from his arms, she realized with a swift shock the loss of all sense of security. She shot a quick glance at him, half terrified, half wistful. But the Tyro was now all for action.

"What clothes do you most need?" he asked sharply.

"Clothes? I don't know." She found it hard to adjust the tumult which had suddenly sprung up within her, to such considerations.

"Shoes and stockings. A heavy coat. Your warmest dress—where is it? What else?"

"What are you going to do?"

"Go back after your things."

"You mustn't! I won't let you. It's dangerous."

"Later it may be. Not now."

She stretched out her hands to him. "Please don't leave me."

He took the imploring little hands in his own firm grip. "Listen. There's no telling what has happened. We may have to go on deck. We may even be ordered to the boats. Warm clothing is an absolute necessity. Think now, and tell me what you need."

She gave him a quick but rather sketchy list. "And your own overcoat and sweater—or I won't let you go. Promise." Her fingers turned in his and caught at them.

"Very well, tyrant. I'll be back in three minutes."

Had he known what was awaiting him he might have promised with less confidence. For there was a dragon in the path in the person of young Mr. Diedrick Sperry, breathing, if not precisely flames, at least, fumes, for he had sat late in the smoking-room, consuming much liquor. At sight of the Tyro, his joke which he had so highly esteemed, returned to his mind.

"Haberdashin' 'round again, hey?" he shouted, blocking the passage halfway down to Stateroom 129. "Where's Cissy Wayne?"

"Safe," said the Tyro briefly.

"Safe be damned! You tell me where before you move a step farther." He stretched out a hand which would have done credit to a longshoreman.

Fight was the last thing that the Tyro wished. More important business was pressing. But as Sperry was blocking the way to the conclusion of that business, it was manifest that he must be disposed of. Here was no time for diplomacy. The Tyro struck at his bigger opponent, the blow falling short. With a shout, the other rushed him, and went right on over his swiftly dropped shoulder, until he felt himself clutched at the knees in an iron grip, and heaved clear of the flooded floor.

The stateroom door opposite swung unlatched. With a mighty effort, the wrestler whirled his opponent clean through it, heard his frame crash into the berth at the back, and slammed the door to after him, only to be apprised, by a lamentable yell in a deep contralto voice, that he had made an unfortunate choice of safe-deposits.

In two leaps he was in room 129 D, whence, peering forth, he beheld his late adversary emerge and speed down the narrow hall in full and limping flight, pursued by Mrs. Charlton Denyse clad in inconsiderable pink, and shrieking vengeance as she splashed. Relieved, through this unexpected alliance, of further interference, the messenger collected a weird assortment of his liege's clothing and an article or two of his own and returned to her. There was no mistaking the gladness of her relief.

"You've done very well," she approved. "Though I don't know that I actually need this lace collar, and I suppose I *could* brave the perils of the deep without that turquoise necklace."

"I took what I could get," explained he. "It's my rule of life."

"Did you obey my orders? Yes, I see you did. Put on your overcoat at once. It's cold. And you're awfully wet," she added, with charming dismay, looking at his feet.

"They'll dry out. There's quite a little water below."

Little Miss Grouch studied him for a moment of half-smiling consideration. "I want to ask you something," she said presently.

"Ask, O Queen, and it shall be answered you."

"Would you have come after me just the same if—if I'd been really a Miss Grouch, and red-nosed, and puffy-faced, and a frump, and homely?"

He took the question under advisement, with a gravity suitable to its import. "Not just the same," he decided, "not as—as anxiously."

"But you'd have come?"

"Oh, yes, I'd have come."

"I thought so." Her voice was strange. There was a pause. "Do you know you're a most exasperating person? It wouldn't make any difference to you who a woman was, if she needed help, whether she was in the steerage—"

He leaped to his feet. "The baby!" he cried, "and his mother. I'd forgotten."

On the word he was gone. Little Miss Grouch looked after him, and there was a light in her eyes which no human being had ever surprised there—and which would have vastly surprised herself had she appreciated the purport of it.

In five minutes he was back, having calmly violated one of the most rigid of ship's rules, in bringing steerage passengers up to the first cabin.

"Here's the Unparalleled Urchin," he announced, "right as a trivet. Here, let's make a little camp." He pulled around a settee, established the frightened but quiet mother and the big-eyed child on it, drew up a chair for himself next to the girl and said, "Now we can wait comfortably for whatever comes."

News it was that came, in the course of half an hour. An official, the genuineness of whose relief was patent, announced that the leak was above water-line, that it was being patched, that the ship was on her way and that there was absolutely no danger, his statement being backed up by the resumed throb of the engines and the sound of many hammers on the port side. Stateroom holders in D and E, however, he added, would best arrange to remain in the saloon until morning.

So the Tyro conveyed his adoptive charges back to the steerage, and returned to his other and more precious charge. There he found Judge Enderby in attendance.

"Isn't there something more I can get from your room?" the Tyro asked of Little Miss Grouch, after he had greeted the judge.

She shook her head with a smile.

"So the dumb has found a tongue, eh?" remarked the lawyer.

"Emergency use only," explained the Tyro.

"Well, my legal advice," pursued the jurist with a reassuring grimace at the girl, "is that you can make hay while the moon shines, for I don't think any officer is going to concern himself with your little affair just at present. But my personal advice," he added significantly, "in the interests of your own peace of mind, is that you go and sit on the rudder the rest of the voyage. Safety first!"

"I think he's an awfully queer old man," pouted Little Miss Grouch, as the judge sauntered away.

"Don't abuse my counsel," said the Tyro.

"He isn't your counsel. He's my counsel. I paid him five whole dollars to be."

"Hoots, lassie! I paid him ten."

"You want my house," said Little Miss Grouch, aggrieved, "and you want my lawyer. Is there anything else of mine you'd like to lay claim to?"

It may have been accident—the unprincipled opportunist of a godling who rules these matters will league himself with any chance—that the Tyro's eyes fell upon her hand, which lay, pink and warmly half-curled in her lap, and remained there. It certainly was not accident that the hand was hastily moved.

"Do you suppose Baby Karl and his mother are safe?" she inquired, in a voice of extreme detachment.

"Just as safe as we are. By the way, you heard what Judge Enderby suggested to me about 'safety first'?"

Her face took on an expression of the severest innocence. "No. Something stupid, I dare say."

"He advised me to go and sit on the rudder for the rest of the voyage."

"Wouldn't it be awfully wet—and lonely?"

"Unspeakably. Particularly the latter."

"Then I wouldn't do it," she counseled.

"I won't," he promised. "But, Miss Grouch, the dry land may be just as lonely as the wet ocean."

"Haven't you any friends in Europe?"

"No. Unless you count Lord Guenn one."

"You never met him until I introduced you, did you?"

"No. But he's asked me to come and visit him at Guenn Oaks."

"Has he! Why?"

The Tyro laughed. "There's something very unflattering about your surprise. Not for my *beaux yeux* alone. It seems he's sort of inherited me from a careless ancestor."

"*I* came to him by marriage."

"So he tells me. Also that you're going to Guenn Oaks."

"Yes."

"Well?"

"Why 'well'? I didn't say anything."

"You didn't. I'm waiting to hear you."

"What?"

"Tell me whether I'm to go or not."

"What have I to do with it?"

"Everything."

"Your servitude ends the moment we touch land."

"It will never end," said the Tyro in a low voice.

Little Miss Grouch peeked up at him from under the fascinating, slanted brows, and immediately regretted her indiscretion. What she saw in his face stirred within her a sweet and tremulous panic, the like of which she had not before experienced.

"Please don't look at me like that," she said petulantly. "What will people think?"

"People are, for once, minding their own businesses, bless 'em."

"Well, anyway, you make me n-n-nervous."

"Am I to come to Guenn Oaks?"

"I'll tell you to-morrow," she fenced.

"To-morrow I shan't be speaking to you."

"Why not?—oh, I forgot. Still, you might write," she dimpled.

"Would you answer?"

"I'll consider it."

"How long would consideration require?"

"Was there ever such a human question-mark! Please, kind sir, I'm awfully tired and sleepy. Won't you let me off now?"

"Forgive me," said the Tyro with such profound contrition that the Wondrous Vision's heart smote her, for she had said, in her quest of means of defense, the thing which most distinctly was not true.

Never had she felt less sleepy. Within her was a terrifying and quivering tumult. She closed her eyes upon the outer world, which seemed now all comprised in one personality. Within the closed lids she had shut the imprint of the tired, lean, alert, dependable face. Within the doors of her heart, which she was now striving to close, was the memory of his protective manliness, of his unobtrusive helpfulness, of the tonic of his frank and healthy humor—and above all of the strength and comfort of his arms as he had caught her up out of the flood. As she mused, the slumber-god crept in behind those blue-veined shutters of thought, and melted her memories into dreams.

While consciousness was still feebly efficient, but control had passed from the surrendering mind, she stretched out a groping hand. The Tyro's closed over it very gently. At the corner of her delicate mouth the merest ghost of a smile flickered and passed. Little Miss Grouch went deep into the land of dreams, with her knight keeping watch and ward over her.

Came then the destroying ogre, in the form of the captain, and passed on; came then the wicked fairy, in the person of Mrs. Charlton Denyse, and passed on, not without some gnashing of metaphorical teeth (her own, I regret to state, she had left in her berth); came also the god from the machine, in the shape of Judge Willis Enderby, with his friend Dr. Alderson, and paused near the group.

"Love," observed the jurist softly, "is nine tenths opportunity and the rest importunity. I hope our young protégé doesn't forget that odd tenth. It's important."

"It seems to me," observed his companion suspiciously, "that you boast considerable wisdom about the tender passion."

The ablest honest lawyer in New York sighed. "I am old who once was young, but *ego in Arcadia fui* and I have not forgotten." Then the two old friends passed on.

HER KNIGHT KEEPING WATCH OVER HER

VII

Seventh day out.
This sea-life is too darned changeable for me.
You never know what next.
It's bad for the nerves—

<small>SMITH'S LOG.</small>

Thus the Tyro, in much perturbation of spirit, at the end of a lonely day. *"Varium et mutabile semper,"* was written, however, not of the sea but of woman. And it was of woman and woman's incomprehensibility that the keeper of the private log was petulantly thinking when he made that entry.

For, far from harrying him about the decks, Little Miss Grouch had now withdrawn entirely from his ken. He had written her once, he had written her twice; he had surreptitiously thrust a third note beneath her door. No answer came to any of his communications. Being comparatively innocent of the way of a maid with a man, the Tyro was discouraged. He considered that he was not being fairly used. And he gloomed and moped and was an object of private mirth to Judge Enderby.

Two perfectly sound reasons accounted for the Joyous Vision's remaining temporarily invisible. The first was that she needed sleep, and Stateroom 129 D, which she had once so despitefully characterized, seemed a very haven of restfulness when, after breakfast, it was reported habitably dried out; the other was a queer and exasperating reluctance to meet the Tyro—yes, even to see him. As the lifting of the embargo on speech was not known to him, she knew herself to be insured against direct address. But the mere thought of meeting him face to face, of having those clear, quiet gray eyes look into hers again, gave her the most mysterious and disquieting sensations.

"I do wish," said Little Miss Grouch to herself, "that his name weren't so perfectly *awful*."

Some thought-demon with a special mission for the persecution of maidens, put it into her head to inquire why she should so vehemently wish this thing. And the trail of that thought plunged her, face-first, into her pillow.

Thereafter she decided that if she went on deck at all that day, it would be with such a surrounding of bodyguard as should keep wandering Daddleskinks quite beyond her range of association. As for his notes, she would answer them when she thought fit. Meantime—as the writer thereof might have been enheartened to know—she put them away in the most private and personal compartment of her trunk, giving each a tender little pat to settle it comfortably into its place.

Doubtless the sun shone that day (the official records said, "Clear with light winds and a calm sea"); doubtless the crippled ship limped happily enough on her way; doubtless there was good food and drink, music and merriment, and the solace of enlivening company aboard. But the snap-shot of the Tyro surreptitiously taken by Judge Enderby—he having borrowed Alderson's traveling-camera for the purpose—showed a face which might suitably have been used as a marginal illustration for that cheerless hymn, "This world is all a fleeting show."

Life had lost all its flavor for the Tyro. He politely accepted Dr. Alderson's invitation to walk, but lagged with so springless a step that the archæologist began to be concerned for his health. At Lord Guenn's later suggestion that squash was the thing for incipient seediness, he tried that, but played a game far too listless for the Englishman's prowess.

In vain did he seek consolation in the society of Karl, the Pride of the Steerage. That intelligent infant wept and would not be comforted because the pretty lady had not come also, and the Tyro was well fain to join him in his lamentations. Only the threatening advance of Diedrick Sperry, with a prominent and satisfactory decoration in dusky blue protruding from his forehead, roused him to a temporary zest in life. Mr. Sperry came, breathing threats and future slaughter, but met a disconcertingly cold and undisturbable gleam of the gray eye.

"If you interfere with me again," said the Tyro, "I'll throw you overboard."

And it was said in such evident good faith that his opponent deemed it best to forget that matter, vaguely suspecting that he had encountered a "professional."

A more fearsome opponent bore down upon the depressed scion of all the Smiths, late that afternoon. Mrs. Charlton Denyse maneuvered him into a curve of the rail, and there held him with her glittering eye.

"I beg your pardon." This, pitched on a flat and haughty level of vocality, was her method of opening the conversation.

The Tyro sought refuge in the example of classic lore. "You haven't offended me," he said, patterning his response upon the White Queen. "Perhaps you're going to," he added apprehensively.

"I am going to talk to you for your own good," was the chill retort.

"Oh, Lord! That's worse."

"Do you see that ship?" The Denyse hand pointed, rigid as a bar, to the south, where the Tyro discerned a thin smudge of smoke.

"I see something."

"That is the Nantasket."

"At this distance I can't deny it," murmured the Tyro.

"Which left New York two days behind us, and is now overhauling us, owing to our accident."

He received this news with a bow.

"On board her is Henry Clay Wayne," she continued weightily.

"Congratulations on your remarkable keenness of vision!" exclaimed the Tyro.

"Don't be an imbecile," said the lady, "I didn't see him. I learned by wireless."

"Rather a specialty of yours, wireless, isn't it?" he queried.

She shot an edged look at him, but his expression was innocence itself. "He will reach England before us."

"Then you don't think he'll board us and make us all walk the plank?" asked the Tyro in an apparent agony of relief.

"Don't get flip—" cried the exasperated lady—"pant," she added barely in time—"with me. Mr. Wayne will be in England waiting for you."

"Anyway, he can't eat me," the Tyro comforted himself. "Shall I hide in the stoke-hole? Shall I disguise myself as a rat and go ashore in the cargo? What do you advise?"

"I advise you to keep away from Miss Wayne."

"Yes. You did that before. At present I'm doing so."

"Then continue."

"I shall, until we reach solid earth."

"There my responsibility will cease. Mr. Wayne will know how to protect his daughter from upstart fortune-hunters."

The Tyro regarded her with an unruffled brow. "Never hunted a fortune in my life. A modest competence is the extent of my ambition, and I've attained that, thanking you for your kind interest."

"In the necktie and suspender business, I suppose," she snapped, enraged at her failure to pierce the foe's armor. "It's a crying scandal that you should thrust yourself on your betters."

This annoyed the Tyro. Not that he allowed Mrs. Denyse to perceive it. With a bland, reminiscent smile he remarked:—

"Speaking of scandals, I observed a young man, rather informally clad, entering Stateroom 144 D at a late hour last night, in some haste."

"Oh!" gasped Mrs. Denyse, and there was murder in her tones.

"He looked to me like young Sperry."

Mrs. Denyse glowed ocular fire.

"And, according to the list, Stateroom 144 D is occupied by Mrs. Charlton Denyse."

Mrs. Denyse growled an ominous, subterranean growl.

"Now, my dear madam, in view of this fact, which I perceive you do not deny" (here the lady gave evidence of having a frenzied protest stuck in her throat like a bone), "I would suggest that you cease chaperoning me and attend to the proprieties in your own case. Hi, Dr. Alderson!" he called to that unsuspecting savant who was passing, "will you look after Mrs. Denyse for a bit? I fear she's ill." And he made his escape.

What Mrs. Denyse said to Dr. Alderson when she regained the power of coherent speech, is beside the purposes of this chronicle. Suffice it to state that he left in some alarm, believing the unfortunate woman to have lost her mind.

The Tyro sought out his deck-chair and relapsed into immitigable boredom. He was not the only person aboard to be dissatisfied with the way affairs were developing. As an amateur Cupid, Judge Enderby had been fancying himself quite decidedly. Noting, however, that there had been absolutely no communication between his two young clients that day, he began to distrust his diplomacy, and he set about the old, familiar problem of administering impetus to inertia. Sad though I am to say it of so eminent a member of the bar, his method perilously approached betrayal of a client's confidence.

It was after his evening set-to at bridge, when, coming on deck for a good-night sniff of air, he encountered the Tyro who was lugubriously contemplating the moon.

"Hah!" he greeted. "How's the dumb palsy?"

"Worse," was the morose reply.

"Haven't seen your pretty little acquaintance about to-day. Have you?"

"No."

"Don't swear at me, young man," reproved the lawyer, mildly.

"I didn't swear at you, sir," said the startled Tyro.

"Not in words, but in tone. Not that I blame you for being put out. At your age, to miss the sun from out of the heavens—and Miss Wayne is certainly a fascinating and dangerous young person. Considering that she is barely twenty-one, it is quite remarkable."

"Remarkable?" repeated the Tyro vaguely.

"Considering that she is barely twenty-one, I said."

The Tyro rubbed his head. Was loneliness befuddling his brain? "I'm afraid I'm stupid," he apologized.

"I'm afraid your fears are well based."

"But—*what's* remarkable?"

"It's remarkable that you should be deaf as well as dumb," retorted the other, testily. "To resume: considering that she is barely twenty-one—not nearly, but *barely* twenty-one, you'll note—"

"You needn't go any further," cried the youth, suddenly enlightened. "Twenty-one is legal age on the high seas?"

"It is."

"Then she's her own mistress and the captain has no more authority over her than over me?"

"So much, I have reason to believe, an eminent legal authority pointed out to the captain yesterday."

"Why didn't that same eminent authority point it out to me before?"

"Before? I object to the implication. I haven't pointed it out to you now. Your own natural, if somewhat sluggish intelligence inferred it from a random remark about a friend's age."

"Does she know it?"

"She does."

"Since when?"

"Since some forty-eight hours."

"Then, why on earth didn't she tell me? She knew I didn't dare speak to her. But she never said a word."

"Give me," began the judge, "five" (here the Tyro reached for his pocket, but the other repudiated the gesture with a wave of the hand) "million dollars, and I wouldn't undertake to guess why any female between the ages of one and one hundred years, does or does not do any given thing. I'm no soothsayer."

"Then I may speak to her to-morrow, without fear of making trouble?"

"You may certainly speak to her—if you can find her. As for trouble, I wouldn't care to answer for you," chuckled the judge. "Good-night to you."

The Tyro sat up late, asking questions of the moon, who, being also of feminine gender, obstinately declined to betray the secrets of the sex.

VIII

Eighth day out.
  Glorious sunshine, a tingling wind, and the ship
    just "inchin' along like a poor inch-worm."
Everything's wrong with the ship; —
  Everything's right with the world.
Perfectly satisfied with the Macgregor hospitality.
She may take all the time she wants,
  so far as I'm concerned —

SMITH'S LOG.

Out of the blue void of a fleckless sky, came whooping at dawn a boisterous wind. All the little waves jumped from their slow-swinging cradles to play with it, and, as they played, became big waves, with all the sportiveness of children and all the power of giants. The Clan Macgregor was their toy.

At first she pretended indifference, and strove to keep the even tenor of her way, regardless of them. But they were too much and too many for her. She began to cripple and jig most painfully for one of her size and dignity. She limped, she wobbled, she squattered, she splashed and sploshed, she reeled hither and thither like an intoxicated old rounder buffeted by a crowd of practical jokers, and she lost time hand over fist, to the vast approval of Mr. Alexander Forsyth Smith. Time was now just so much capital to his hopes.

The tonic seduction of the gale was too much for Little Miss Grouch. This was no day for a proven sailor to be keeping between decks. Moreover, the maiden panic was now somewhat allayed. The girl's emotions, after the first shock of the surprise and the resentment of the hitherto untouched spirit, had come under control. She could now face a Daddleskink or a regiment of Daddleskinks, unmoved, so she felt—with proper support. Hence, like the Tyro, she was on deck early.

So they met. As in the mild and innocent poem of Victorian days, "'twas in a crowd." Little Miss Grouch had provided the crowd, and the Tyro simply added one to it. He was fain if not wholly content to stay in the background and bide his chance.

Now Little Miss Grouch, ignorant of the fact that her high-priced counsel had betrayed her cause, marveled and was disturbed when the Tyro approached, greeted her, and straightway dropped into the fringe of Society as constituted by herself for the occasion. Was he deliberately, in the face of his own belief that imprisonment would be the penalty of any communication between her and himself, willing to risk her liberty? If so, he was not the man she had taken him for. Little Miss Grouch's ideal was rocking a bit on his pedestal.

Patience was not one of the young lady's virtues. On the other hand, the compensating quality of directness was. "Do It Now" was her prevailing motto. She wanted to know what her slave meant by his abrupt change of attitude, and she wanted to know at once. But her methods, though prompt, were not wholly lacking in finesse. Out of her surrounding court she appointed Judge Enderby and Lord Guenn escorts for the morning promenade, and picked up Dr. Alderson on the way.

Be it duly set down to the credit of the Joyous Vision's solider qualities, that old men found her as interesting a companion, though in a different way, as did young men. By skillful management, she led the conversation to the house on the Battery, with the anticipated result that Judge Enderby (all innocent, wily old fox though he was, that he was playing her game) suggested the inclusion of the other claimant in the conference. The Tyro was summoned and came.

"The charge against you," explained the judge, "is contumaciousness in that you still insist on coveting a property which is claimed by royalty, under the divine right of queens."

"I'd be glad to surrender it," said the Tyro meekly, "but there seems to be a species of family obligation about it."

"Obligation or no obligation, you know you can't have it," declared the lady.

"I rather expect to, though."

"When papa says he'll get a thing, he always gets it," she informed him with lofty confidence, "and he has promised me that house."

"Then I'm afraid that this is the time his promise goes unfulfilled," said Judge Enderby.

She turned to him with incredulously raised brows.

"Alderson knows the old records; he's seen the option—it's a queer old document, by the way, but sound legally—and can swear to it."

"The only loose joint is the exact plan of the original property," observed the archæologist.

"And that is in the picture at Guenn Oaks," contributed Lord Guenn.

"Why are you all against me?" cried Little Miss Grouch in grieved amazement.

"Not against you at all," said Judge Enderby. "It's simply a matter of the best claim. Besides, you, who have everything in the world, would you turn this poor homeless young wanderer out of a house that he's never been in?"

"Except by ancestral proxy," qualified Dr. Alderson.

"How *mean* of you!" She turned the fire of denunciatory eyes upon the archæologist. "You told me with your own lips that no family named Daddleskink was ever connected in the remotest degree with the house. You said the idea was as absurd as the name."

"So it is."

"Yet you turn around and declare that Mr. Daddleskink's claim is good."

"*Whose* claim?"

"Mr. Daddleskink's." She indicated the Tyro with a scornful gesture. "Oh," she added, noting the other's obvious bewilderment, "I see you didn't know his real name."

"I? I've known him and his name all his life."

"And it isn't Daddleskink?"

The learned archæologist lapsed against the rail and gave way to wild mirth. "Wh—where on earth d-d-did you gu-gu-get such a notion?" he quavered, when he could speak.

"He told me, himself."

"I? Never!" The Tyro's face was as that of a babe for innocence.

"*You—didn't—tell—me—your—name—was—Daddleskink?*"

"Certainly not. I simply asked if you didn't think it a misfortune to be named Daddleskink, and you jumped to the conclusion that it was my name and my misfortune."

"Perhaps you didn't tell me, either, that your friends called you 'Smith,'" she said ominously.

"So they do."

"Why should they call you 'Smith' if your name isn't Daddleskink?" she demanded, with an effect of unanswerable logic.

"Because my name *is* Smith."

"Permit me to present," said Lord Guenn, who had been quietly but joyously appreciative of the duel, "my ancestral friend, Mr. Alexander Forsyth Smith."

"Why didn't you tell me your real name?" Little Miss Grouch's offended regard was fixed upon the Tyro.

"Well, you remember, you made fun of the honorable cognomen of Smith when we first met."

"That is no excuse."

"And you were mysterious as an owl about your own identity."

"I could see no occasion for revealing it." The delicately modeled nose was now quite far in the air.

"So I thought I'd furnish a really interesting name for you to amuse yourself with. I'm sorry you don't care for it."

Little Miss Grouch's limpid and lofty consideration passed from the anxious physiognomy of the speaker to the mirthful countenances of the other three.

"I'm not sure that I shall ever speak to any of you again," she stated, and, turning her back, marched away from them with lively resentment expressed in every supple line of her figure.

"Young man," said Judge Enderby to his client, as the male quartette, thus cavalierly dismissed, passed on, "will you take the advice of an old man?"

"Have I paid for it?" inquired the Tyro.

"You have not. Gratis advice, this. The most valuable kind."

"Shoot, sir."

"Don't let two blades of grass grow under your feet where one grew before."

"But—"

"—me no buts. Half an hour I give you. If you haven't found the young lady in that time I discard you."

Opportunity for successful concealment on shipboard is all but limitless. Hence the impartial recorder must infer that the efforts of Little Miss Grouch to elude pursuit were in no way excessive. A quarter of an hour sufficed for the searcher to locate his object in a sunny nook on the boat-deck. He approached and stood at attention. For several moments she ignored his presence. In point of fact she pretended not to see him. He shifted his position. She turned her head in the reverse direction and pensively studied the sea.

The Tyro sighed.

Little Miss Grouch frowned.

The Tyro coughed gently.

Little Miss Grouch scowled.

The Tyro lapsed to the deck and curled his legs under him.

Little Miss Grouch turned upon him a baleful eye. But her glance wavered: at least, it twinkled. Her little jaw was set, it is true. At the corner of her mouth, however, dimpled a suspicious and delicious quiver. Perhaps the faintest hint of it crept into her voice to mollify the rigor of the tone in which she announced:

"I came here to be alone."

"We are," said the Tyro. "At last!" he added with placid satisfaction.

"Well, really!" For the moment it was all that came to her, as offset to this superb impudence. "Go away, at once," she commanded presently.

"I can't."

"Why not?"

"I'm lame," he said plaintively. "Pity the poor cripple."

"A little while ago you were deaf; then dumb. And now—By the way," she cried, struck with a sudden reminiscence, "what has become of your dumbness?"

"Cured."

"A miracle. Listen then. And stop looking at that crack in the deck as if you'd lost your last remaining idea down it."

"To look up is dangerous."

"Where's the danger?"

"Dangerous to my principles," he explained. "You see, you are somewhat less painful to the accustomed eye than usual to-day, and if I should so far forget my principles as to mention that fact—"

"You haven't a principle to your name! You're untruthful—"

"Ah, come, Little Miss Grouch!"

"Deceitful—"

"As to that Smith matter—"

"And most selfishly inconsiderate of me."

"Of you!" cried the Tyro, roused to protest.

116

"Certainly. Or you wouldn't be exposing me to imprisonment in my cabin by talking to me."

THE TYRO CURLED HIS LEGS UNDER HIM

"Nothing doing," said he comfortably. "That little joke is played out."

"How did you know?"

Loyalty forbade the Tyro to betray his ally. "That you were of age, you mean, and couldn't be treated like a child?" he fenced.

"Yes."

"Well, when you spoke of the house on the Battery being deeded over to you, I knew that you must have reached your majority! The rest was simple to figure out."

"Oh, dear!" she mourned. "It was such fun chasing you around the ship!"

"Yes? Well, I've emulated the startled fawn all I'm going to this trip."

"What's your present rôle?"

"Meditation upon the wonder of existence."

"Do you find it good?"

"Existence? That depends. Am I to come to Guenn Oaks?"

"I'm sure you'd be awfully in the way there," she said petulantly. "You've been a perfect nuisance for the last two days."

"My picturesqueness has gone glimmering, now that I'm only a Smith instead of a Daddleskink. Why, oh, why must these lovely illusions ever perish!"

"*You* killed cock-robin," she accused.

"Not at all. It was Dr. Alderson with his misplaced application of the truth."

"Anyway, I don't find you nearly so entertaining, now that you're plain Mr. Smith."

"Nor I you as Miss Cecily Wayne, equally plain if not plainer."

"In that case," she suggested with a mock-mournful glance from beneath the slanted brows, "this acquaintance might as well die a painless death."

"But for one little matter that you've forgotten."

"And that?"

"The Magnificent Manling of the Steerage."

"So I had forgotten! Let's go make our call on him. We must not neglect him a moment longer."

The Tyro leaped to his feet and they ran, hand in hand like two children, down to their point of observation of the less favored passengers. They spent a lively half-hour with the small Teuton, at the end of which Little Miss Grouch issued imperative commands to the Tyro to the effect that he was to wait at the pier when they got in, and see to it that mother and child were safely forwarded to the transfer.

"Yessum," said the Tyro meekly. "Anything further?"

"I'll let you know," she returned, royally. "You may wire me when the commission is executed. Perhaps, if you carry it through very nicely, I'll let you come to Guenn Oaks."

"Salaam, O Empress," returned the Tyro, executing a most elaborate Oriental bow, the concluding spiral of which almost involved him in Mrs. Charlton Denyse's suddenly impending periphery.

Mrs. Denyse retired three haughty paces.

"I wish to speak to Miss Wayne," she announced with a manner which implied that she did not wish and never again would wish to speak to Miss Wayne's companion.

"With me?" asked Little Miss Grouch, bland surprise in her voice.

"Yes. I have a message."

Little Miss Grouch waited.

"A private message," continued the lady.

"Is it very private? You know Mr. Daddleskink-Smith, I believe?"

"I've seen Mr. Daddleskink-Smith," frigidly replied the lady, mistaking the introducer's hesitation for a hyphen, "if that is what he calls himself now."

"It isn't," said the Tyro. "You know, Mrs. Denyse, I've always held that the permutation of names according to the taste of the inheritor, is one of the most interesting phases of social ingenuity."

Mrs. Charlton Denyse, relict of the late Charley Dennis, turned a deep Tyrian purple. "If you would be good enough—" she began, when the girl broke in:—

"Is your message immediate, Mrs. Denyse?"

"It is from my cousin, Mr. Van Dam."

"To me?" cried the girl.

"No. To me. By wireless. But it concerns you."

"In that case I don't think I'm interested," said the girl, her color rising. "You must excuse me." And she walked on.

"Then the gentlemanly spider on the hot griddle loses," murmured the Tyro.

"I don't know whom you mean," said the girl, obstinately.

"I mean that your foot-destroying 'Never-never-never' holds good."

"Yes," she replied. "I did think I *might* marry him once. But now," she added pensively and unguardedly, "I know I never could."

The Tyro's heart came into his throat—except that portion of it which looked out of his eyes.

"Why?"

A flame rose in Little Miss Grouch's cheeks, and subsided, leaving her shaking.

"Why?" He had halted her beside the rail, and was trying to look into her face, which was averted toward the sea, and quivering with panic of the peril suddenly become imminent again.

Lord Guenn, approaching along the deck, furnished Little Miss Grouch an inspiration, the final flash of hope of the hard-pressed.

"Shut your eyes," she bade her terrifying slave.

"What for?"

"Obey!"

"They're shut."

"Tight?"

"Under sealed orders."

Little Miss Grouch made a swift signal to the approaching Englishman, and executed a silent maneuver.

"Count three," she directed breathlessly, "before you ask again or open your eyes."

"One—two—three," said the Tyro slowly. "*Why?*"

"Hanged if I know, my dear fellow," replied Lord Guenn, upon whose trim elegance the Tyro's discomfited vision rested.

Little Miss Grouch had vanished.

IX

Ninth day out
  Sixty days has September,
  April, June and November.
  From January until May
  The rain it raineth every day.
  All the rest have thirty-one
  Without a single gleam of sun.
  If any should have thirty-two,
  They'd be dull and dirty, too!

ADAPTED BY SMITH FOR SMITH'S LOG.

Rain, fog, mist, drizzle, more rain. Such was the waste world through which the Clan Macgregor wallowed. Other ships passed her, hooting as they went. Small craft began to loom up under her massive bows, and slide away from beneath her towering stern, always eluding Fate, as it seemed, by miraculous inches. And slower and ever slower moved the sea-mammoth, lugubriously trumpeting her distress and dismay at the plight in which she found herself.

Thus and no otherwise would the Tyro have vented his grief and chagrin, had he possessed competent vocal organs, more lost and befogged than the ship which bore him and his sorrow to an alien land. For breakfast had come and gone, and then luncheon and dinner, and nowhere had he caught so much as a glimpse of Little Miss Grouch. At ten o'clock that night he was standing immersed in gloom, within and without, staring out over the rail into a world of blackness. Far out in the void, a bell tolled. The Tyro resumed his purposeless promenade, meditating cheerlessly upon buried hopes.

Now, were individuals required, as are craft, to carry fog signals, this maritime record might be something other than it is. The collision was head on, and the impact severe. The lighter craft recoiled against the rail.

"Oh!" she said.

"You!" cried the Tyro, with the voice of glad tidings.

"How you frightened me!" she said, but the tone indicated more of relief, not to say content, than alarm.

"I'm sorry. Where have you been all day?"

"Packing."

"Oh!" There was a pause. Then: "Lord Guenn doesn't know."

"Doesn't know what?"

"Doesn't know why. I asked him, you know. When you—er—disappeared. So I have to ask you again. Why?"

"Aren't you afraid that when you die you'll change into a question-mark?"

"Not at all. I intend to be answered before I die. Long before. One—two—three; why?"

But she was ready for the question now. "About Mr. Van Dam, you mean?" said she with elaborate carelessness. "Oh, well, you see, I'd be Mrs. Denyse's cousin in that case and, after a week of her, I've concluded that it isn't worth the price."

"Hard-hearted Parent will be displeased."

"I'm afraid so. Perhaps he'll cut me off with a shilling."

"I hope so."

"Now, that isn't a bit kind of you," she complained. "I'm not fitted for poverty. Not that it would be literally a shilling. But to have to do everything on twelve thousand a year—"

"How much?"

"That's all I can call my really own."

"And you consider that insufficient?" asked the Tyro, in a queer, strained voice.

"Not as long as papa pays my principal bills," she explained. "But of course, to live on—" An expressive shrug furnished the conclusion.

"For some years I lived on less than a tenth of it," said he.

"No! It couldn't be done."

"Don't you know anything at all about life?" he demanded, almost angrily.

"Of course I do. But I don't bother about money and such things."

"I do. I've had to all my life. Even now, when I consider myself very well off, I can make only a little more than the income which you consider mere pin-money."

"Yet you can buy houses on the Battery," she insinuated.

"Only through the option that gives me the inside track. And even that will make a huge hole in my pile."

"Ah, well," she said petulantly. "I don't see what difference it makes. Anyway, I'm bored. Aren't you going to be any more amusing than this at Guenn Oaks?"

"I'm not coming to Guenn Oaks."

"Who are you to say what you are or are not going to do—Slave?" she said with her most imperious air.

At the tone, he rallied a difficult smile. "I'm the Honest Workingman. Whereas you are—" he spread his hands out in a suave gesture, which was exceedingly displeasing to Little Miss Grouch—"a mirage."

"A mirage?" she repeated.

"The Eternally Unattainable."

"Long words always make my head ache."

"I'll state it mathematically. If you concentrate your powerful intellect upon the problem you will perceive that two plus two equals four."

"In that faith I live and die! But what it has to do with Bertie Guenn's invitation—"

"The sum proves up equally when raised to thousands, or millions."

"What concern has a Perfect Pig with figures?" she asked wistfully, and lifted a hesitant hand in the darkness.

It fell lightly on his arm. In the soft gloom her face glimmered, dimly warm to his vision, upturned to his. The fog covered much that might otherwise have been seen, but failed to smother what might have been (and in fact was, as Judge Enderby and Dr. Alderson, turning the angle of the deck, halted and tactfully melted away) heard. To wit:—

"Oh!" in a feminine and tremulous pitch.

"Forgive me," said the Tyro hoarsely. "That was for good-bye."

Was it a detaining hand that went forth in the darkness? If so, it failed of its purpose, for the Tyro had gone.

Then and there Little Miss Grouch proceeded to pervert a proverb.

"Man proposes," she observed to herself, philosophically. "Maybe not always, though. But, anyway, woman disposes. *I* don't think that was *really* good-bye."

Behold now a complete reversal of conditions from the initial night of the voyage. For now it was the Tyro who went to bed, miserable and at odds with a hostile world; whereas Little Miss Grouch dreamed of a morrow, new, glorious, and irradiated with a more splendid adventurousness than her slave had ever previsioned.

LAND HO!

Land Ho!
  A fool for luck went
    a-fishing in the Atlantic
    with his heart for bait — and
    caught the
    Goddess of the Realm of Dreams.
I have sailed out of the
    Port of Chance, across
    the Ocean of Golden hopes,
    straight into the Haven
    of All-Joy —
And so, Journey's End
    in the good old way —

SMITH'S LOG.

Blue-gray out of pearl-gray mist rose the shores of old England. Long before the sun, the Tyro was up and on deck, looking with all his eyes, a little awed, a little thrilled, as every man of the true American blood who honors his country must be at first sight of the Motherland. Slowly, through an increasing glow that lighted land and water alike, the leviathan of the deep made her ponderous progress to the hill-encircled harbor. A step that halted at the Tyro's elbow detached his attention.

"What do you think of it?" asked Lord Guenn.

The eyes of Alexander Forsyth Smith rested for a moment on a toy lighthouse and passed to the trim shore, where a plaything locomotive was pulling a train of midget box-cars with the minimum of noise and effort.

"It's like Fairyland," he said, in a voice unconsciously modulated to the peace of the scene. "So tiny and neatly beautiful."

"Yes; it hasn't the overwhelming magnificence of New York Harbor. But it's England."

"And you're gladder to get back to it than you'd confess, for shame of sentimentalizing," said the other shrewdly, having marked the note of deep content in that "it's England."

"One doesn't climb the rail and sing 'Rule, Britannia.'"

"It's a matter of temperament and training. Inside, I suppose, every decent man feels the same about his own country, allowing for racial differences. I don't suppose, though, you'd have quite the same sensation if you were an American returning home after a long absence."

"Good Lord, no!" was the unguarded reply.

The Tyro laughed outright. "For once I've pierced the disguise of your extremely courteous cosmopolitanism, and behold! there's John Bull underneath, rampantly sure that nobody can be a really justified patriot except an Englishman."

"Confound you and your traps!" retorted the young peer, ruefully. "Ah, I say, Cecily!" he cried as Little Miss Grouch appeared, looking, in her long soft traveling-coat, rather lovelier (so the Tyro considered within himself) than any human being has any right to look.

She came over to the rail, giving the Tyro the briefest flutter of a glance to accompany her "Good-morning, Mr. Smith."

"I appeal to you," continued Lord Guenn. "You're a cosmopolitan —"

"Indeed, I'm not! I'm an American," said the young lady with vigor.

"Heaven preserve us! You Yankees are all alike. You may be as mild and deprecatory as you please at home; one sniff of foreign air, and up goes the Stars and Stripes. Very well, I withdraw the appeal. To change the subject, when are you coming to us? Laura will be on the tender and she'll want to know."

"Dad will also be on the tender," observed Little Miss Grouch, "and he'll want to know, oh, heaps of things!"

"True enough! We'll keep out of the way of your affecting reunion. Lady Guenn's got a stateroom, Smith, in case it might rain. Come around and meet her. Unless I'm mistaken, the tender's putting out now."

"Oh!" cried Little Miss Grouch. "That adorable kiddie! I nearly forgot him. Don't forget, please," she added to the Tyro, "you promised to look after them and see that they got on the right train."

"Steerage passengers come in later," said Lord Guenn. "Hullo! There's your pater, on the upper deck of the tender. Doesn't look particularly stern and unforgiving, does he? Perhaps you'll get off with your life, after all."

Little Miss Grouch turned rather white, and shot an appealing look at the Tyro, correctly interpreting which, he wandered away.

When he next saw her, she was in the arms of a square-faced grizzled man, and manifestly quite content to be there. The tender was swaying alongside in a strong tide-rip and the Tyro himself was making the passage between the two craft carefully but jerkily, in the wake of Alderson and Enderby. Once on the small boat he separated himself from his companions, found a secluded spot at the rail, well aft, and tactfully turned his back upon the Grouch group.

Evolutionists assert that we all possess some characteristic, however vague, of all the forms into which the life-stock has differentiated. Upon this theory the Tyro must have had in his make-up a disproportionate share of the common house-fly, which, we are taught, rejoices in eyes all around its head. For, though he sedulously averted his face from the pair in whom his interest centered, he was perfectly aware of what they were doing.

First Little Miss Grouch glanced at him and said something. Then her father glared at him and said something. Then she turned toward him again and made another remark. Then the disgruntled parent glowered more fiercely and said a worse thing than he had said before. Then both of them regarded him until his ears flushed and swelled to their farthest tips.

All of which was a triumph of the visual imagination. As a matter of fact they weren't talking about him at all. Little Miss Grouch was afraid to. And her stern parent didn't even know who he was. The subject of their conversation was, largely, the Battery Place house.

Still continuing to imagine a vain thing, the Tyro felt the gentlest little pressure on his arm.

"Such a deep-brown, brown study!" said Little Miss Grouch's gay little voice, at his elbow.

The Tyro turned with a sigh, quickly succeeded by a smile. It was very hard not to smile, just for pure joy of the eye, when Little Miss Grouch was in the foreground.

"Why the musing melancholy?" she pursued.

"I'm coming out of Fairyland into the Realm of Realities," he explained. "And I don't believe in realities any more."

"I'm a reality," she averred.

"No." He shook his head. "You're a figment. I made you up, myself, in a burst of creative genius."

"Just like that? Right out of your head?"

"Out of my heart," he corrected.

"Then why not have moulded me nearer to the heart's desire?" she queried cunningly. "Do you still think I'm homely?"

He shut his eyes firmly. "I do."

"And cross?"

"A regular virago."

"And ugly, and messy and an idiot—"

"Hold on! You're double-crossing the indictment. I'm the offended idiot," declared the Tyro, opening his eyes upon her.

She took advantage of his indiscretion.

"*Am* I red-nosed?"

"You are. At least, you will be when you cry again."

"I'll cry straight off this minute, if you don't promise to take it all back."

"I'll promise—the instant we touch shore."

There was a gravity in his tone that banished her mischief.

"Perhaps I don't really want you to take it back," she said wistfully.

"Ah, but with firm earth under our feet once more, and realities all around us—"

"There's Guenn Oaks. That's on the very borders of Elfland. Don't you think Bertie looks like a Pixie?"

"I'm not going to Guenn Oaks."

"Not if I say my very prettiest 'please'?"

From those pleading lips and eyes the Tyro turned away. Instantly there was a piercing squeak of greeting from across the narrow strip of water.

"It's the Beatific Baby!" cried Little Miss Grouch. "How did he ever get there? Oh! Oh!! Get him, some one!"

Near an opening at the rail of the ship some of the third-class luggage had been left. Upon this the Pride of the Steerage had clambered and was there perilously balancing, while he waved his hands at his departing friends. There was a deeper-toned answering cry to Little Miss Grouch's appeal, as the mother, leaping to the rail, ran swiftly along it, seized and hurled her child back, and, with the effort, plunged overboard herself.

By the time she had touched the water, the Tyro's overcoat and coat were on the deck and his hands on the rail.

"Take that life-preserver," he said, with swift quietness to Little Miss Grouch. "As soon as you see me get her, throw it as far beyond us as you can. You understand? Beyond. There she is. *Damn!!*"

For Little Miss Grouch's arms had closed desperately around his shoulders. With his wrestler's knowledge, he could have broken that hold in a second's fraction, but that would have been to fling her against the rail, possibly over it. He twisted until his face almost touched hers.

"Let me go!"

In all her pampered life Miss Cecily Wayne had never before been addressed in that tone or anything remotely resembling it, by man, woman, or child. Her grip relaxed. She shrank back, appalled.

For perhaps a second she had checked him, and in that second the huddle of blue had drifted almost abreast. It was an easy leap from where the Tyro stood. One foot was on the rail, when he staggered aside from an impact very different from the feminine assault. Mr.

Henry Clay Wayne had turned from an absorbing conversation with Mrs. Denyse in time to see his daughter in hand-to-hand combat with a man. Observing the man now about to precipitate himself into the sea, he formulated the theory of an attempted robbery and escape, and acted with the promptitude which had made him famous in Wall Street. As he was a decidedly husky one hundred-and-seventy-pounds' worth, his arrival notably interfered with the Tyro's projects.

Now the Tyro's naturally equable temper had been disturbed by the other encounter, and this one loosed its bonds. Here was no softening consideration of sex. Who the interferer was, the Tyro knew not, nor cared. He drove an elbow straight into the midsection of the enemy, lashed out with a heel which landed square on the most sensitive portion of the shin, broke the relaxed hold with one effort, and charged like a bull through the crowd now lining the rail at the stern curve,—and stopped dead, as a general shout, part cheers, part laughter, arose. The woman was ploughing through the water with great overhand strokes. In a few seconds she stood on the tender's deck, while the crowd congratulated and questioned.

"I'm a feesh," she explained, pointing to a crudely embroidered dolphin on her sleeve, which, as Dr. Alderson explained, meant that she had undergone the famous swimming test in her own German town of Dessau on the Mulde.

Meantime two dukes, a ship's pilot, a negro pugilist, a goddess of grand opera, a noted aviator, and some scores of lesser people looked on in amazement at the third richest man in America hopping on one foot like an inebriated and agonized crane, with his other shin clasped in his hands, and making faces which an amateur photographer hastened to snap, subsequently suppressing them for reasons of humanity and art.

Several people, including Mrs. Charlton Denyse with two red spots on her cheeks besides what she had put there herself, endeavored to explain to the Tyro just what species of high treason he had committed by his assault, but he was in no mood for gratuitous information, and removed himself determinedly from their vicinity. Presently Judge Enderby appeared upon his horizon.

"His leg isn't broken," he announced.

"Whose leg?"

"That of the gentleman you so brutally assaulted. He wants to see you."

"Tell him to go to the devil."

"Oh, I wouldn't do that," soothed the legal veteran, his face twinkling.

"All right. Bring him here and I'll tell him."

"Even though he is Little Miss Grouch's father?"

"What!"

"Precisely. Now, will you go to him?"

"No."

"When you employ one of the highest-priced counsel in America," observed the old man plaintively, "while it isn't essential that you should receive his advice with any degree of courtesy —"

"I really beg your pardon, Judge Enderby. The fact is, my temper has been a little ruffled —"

"Calm it down until you need it again and come with me." The judge tucked an arm under the Tyro's, who presently found himself being studied by a handsomely grim face, somewhat humanized by an occasional twinge of pain. The owner of the face acknowledged Judge Enderby's introduction and waited. The Tyro likewise acknowledged Judge Enderby's introduction and waited. Mr. Wayne was waiting for the Tyro to apologize. The Tyro hadn't the faintest notion of apologizing, and, had he known that it was expected, would have been more exasperated than before, since he considered himself the aggrieved party. Finding silence unproductive, the magnate presently broke it.

"You were going in after that woman?"

"Yes."

"Did you know her?"

"Yes."

"Where?"

"On shipboard."

"Oh! She was the one you and my daughter used to pamper, in the steerage. Mrs. Denyse told me. So you thought you'd be a Young Hero, eh?"

The Tyro caught Judge Enderby's eye, and, reading therein an admonition, preserved his temper and his silence.

"Well, I rather spoiled your little game. And you pretty near ruined my digestion with your infernal elbow."

The Tyro smiled an amiable smile.

"Did you know who I was when you kicked me?"

"No," answered the Tyro in such a tone that the elder man grinned.

"Nor care either, eh?"

"No. I'd have punched you in the eye if I'd had time."

"Don't apologize. You did your best. Now that you do know who I am—"

"I don't. Except that you're the father of Little Miss Grouch."

"Of who—um!" demanded the other, rescuing his grammar from his surprise barely in time to save its fair repute.

The Tyro had the grace to blush. "It's just a foolish nickname," he said.

"Particularly inappropriate, I should say. By the way, your own name seems to be a matter of some doubt. What do you call yourself?"

"Smith."

"By what right?"

"Birthright. If it comes to rights, where is your license to practice cross-examination?"

"Mrs. Charlton Denyse says that your real name is Daddleskink."

"Well, it won't seriously handicap her popularity with me to have her think so."

"Mrs. Charlton Denyse says that your attentions to my daughter have been so marked as to compromise her."

"Mrs. Charlton Denyse is a—well, she's a woman."

"Otherwise you'd punch *her* in the eye?"

"I'd scratch all the new paint off her," said the Tyro virulently.

"My clerk had an awful time with that name of yours. He thought it was code. What's your occupation, Mr. Smith?"

"Answering questions. Have you got many more to ask?"

"I have. Are you a haberdasher?"

"Don't answer," advised Judge Enderby, in his profoundest tones, "if it tends to incriminate or degrade you."

"Hullo!" cried Mr. Wayne. "Where do you come in?"

"I am Mr. Smith's counsel."

"The devil you are!"

"Therefore my presence is strictly professional."

Now, Mr. Henry Clay Wayne was a tolerably shrewd judge of humankind. To be sure, the Tyro was of a species new to him. Hence he had gone cautiously, testing him for temper and poise. At this point he determined upon what he would have described as "rough-neck work."

"How much will he take, Enderby?"

"For what?"

"To quit."

With admirable agility for one of his age, Judge Enderby jumped in front of the Tyro. He had seen, underneath the rebellious side-curl which came down across the youth's temple, a small vein swell suddenly and purply.

"Wayne," said he over his shoulder, "you'd better apologize."

"What for?"

"To save your life. I think my client is about to drop you over the rail, and I can't conscientiously advise him not to."

"No, I'm not," said the Tyro, with an effort. "But I want to hear that again."

"What?" inquired Mr. Wayne.

"That—that offer of a bribe."

"No bribe at all. A straightforward business proposition."

"So that's your notion of business," said the Tyro slowly.

"Well, why not?" Bland innocence overspread the magnate's features as if in a layer. "I ask you to name your price for quitting your pretended claim—"

"I don't pretend any claim!"

"—to a house, which—"

"A house?"

"Certainly. On Battery Place."

"That isn't what you meant," bluntly accused the lawyer.

"Of course it isn't." There was an abrupt and complete change of voice and expression. "My boy, I suppose you think you're in love with my daughter."

The Tyro found this man suddenly a very likable person.

"Think!" he exclaimed.

"Well, if you think so hard enough, you are. And I suppose you want to marry her?"

"I'd give the heart out of my body for her."

"Do you know anything about the kind of girl she is? The life she leads? The things and people that make life for her? The sort of world she lives in?"

"Not very much."

"I suppose not. Well, son, I make up my mind quickly about people. You strike me as something of a man. But I'm afraid you haven't got the backing to carry out this contract."

"We are prepared to show a reasonable income," declared Judge Enderby, "with a juster prospect of permanence than—well, for example, than Wall Street affords, at present."

"Possibly. Of course I could find our young friend here an ornamental and useless position in my office—"

"No, thank you," said the Tyro.

"No. I'd supposed not. Well, Mr. Smith, to keep that amiable young lady running at the rate of speed which she considers legal, trims fifty thousand a year down so fine that I could put the remainder in the plate on New Year's Sunday without a pang."

"Fifty thousand!" gasped the Tyro.

"Oh, the modern American girl is a high-priced luxury. Are you worth a million dollars?"

"No."

"See any prospect of getting a million?"

"Not the slightest."

"Well, do you think it would be fair to a girl like Cecily, with an upbringing which—"

"Which imbecility and snobbery have combined to make the worst imaginable," cut in Judge Enderby.

"I don't say you're wrong. But it's what she's had. That kind of life is no longer a luxury to her. It's a necessity."

"Twaddle!" observed the judge.

"Have it your own way," allowed the father patiently. "But there's the situation," he added to the Tyro. "What are you going to do with it?"

The Tyro looked him between the eyes. "The best I can," said he, and walked away.

"Now, Enderby," said the great financier, following him with his glance, "it's up to the boy and the girl."

"You've killed him off."

"Not if I know Cecily. She's got a good deal of her mother in her. I've always known it would be once and forever with her. And I'm afraid this boy is the once."

"It might be worse," suggested the lawyer dryly.

"Yes. I've made inquiries. But what can a man know about things?" The great man's regard drifted out into the gray distance of the open sea. "Ah, if I had her mother back again!"

"The boy is fine and honorable and manful, Wayne," said the old lawyer. "To be sure, you'll never make a Wall Street dollar-hound out of him —"

"Heaven knows I don't want to."

"But he'll play his part in the world and play it well. I've come to think a good deal of that boy. I wish I were as sure of the girl."

"Cecily? Don't you worry about her." The father chuckled pridefully. "She's got stuff in her. I'd trust her to start the world with as I did with her mother."

What of Little Miss Grouch, while all these momentous happenings were in progress? Events had piled up on her sturdy little nerves rather too fast even for their youthful strength. The emotional turmoil of which the Tyro was the cause, the tension of meeting her father again, and, on top of these, the startling occurrences on the deck of the tender had stretched her endurance a little beyond its limit, and it was with a sense of grateful refuge that she had betaken herself to the hospitality of Lady Guenn's cabin. What transpired between the two women is no matter for the pen of a masculine chronicler. Suffice it to note that Lord Guenn, surcharged with instructions to be casual, set out to find the Tyro, and, having found him, blurted out:—

"I say, Smith, Cecily's in our cabin. If I were you I'd lose no time getting there. It's the only one on the port side aft."

No time was lost by the Tyro. He found Cecily alone. At sight of her face, his heart gave one painful thump, and shriveled up.

"You've been crying," he said.

"I haven't!" she denied. "And if I have, there's enough to make me cry."

"What was it?" was his sufficiently lame rejoinder.

"I imagine if you'd seen your father beaten and kicked as I saw mine—"

"I didn't know who it was."

"But if you had been shaken and cursed, yourself—"

"Cursed? Who cursed you?"

"You did."

"I!"

"You said, 'D-d-damn you, let me go!'"

"I did *not*. I simply told you to let me go."

"Well you might as well have said 'Damn you!' You meant it," whimpered Little Miss Grouch.

"She might have been drowned," said the Tyro.

"So might you. I saved your life by not letting you go in after her. And you haven't a spark of gratitude."

"Well," began the Tyro, astounded at this sudden turn of strategy, "I *am—*"

"Go on and curse some more," she advised. "I suppose you'd have kicked *me* if I hadn't let go."

He stared at her, speechless.

"Now you've made me cu-cu-cry again. And my nose is all red. *Isn't* my nose all red? Say 'Yes.'"

"Yes," said the bewildered young man, obediently.

"And I'm hoarse as a crow. *Am* I? Say it!"

"Y-y-yes," he stammered.

"And I'm homely and frowsy, and dowdy and horrid and a perfect mess. Am I a mess? Say—"

"*No!*" The rebel in the Tyro broke bonds. "You're the loveliest and most adorable and sweetest thing on this earth, and I love you."

"I—I think you might have said it before," said Little Miss Grouch in a very wee voice.

"I'd no business to say it at all. But I simply couldn't go without—"

"Go?" she cried, startled. "Where?"

"Away. It doesn't matter where."

"Away from me?"

"Yes."

She faced him with leveled eyes, tearless now, and infinitely pleading.

"You couldn't do that," she said.

"I must."

"After—after last night, on deck? And—and now—what you've just said?"

"I can't help it, dear," he said miserably. "I've been talking with your father."

"Is it—is it our money?"

"Yes."

"Are you a coward?" she flashed. "Afraid of what people would say?"

"Afraid of what you yourself would feel when you found yourself missing the things you've been used to so long."

"What do I care for those things? It's just a sort of snobbery in you. Oh, I'd have married you when I thought your name was

Daddleskink!" she cried, with flaming face. "And now because we're different from what you thought, you—you—"

"You're not making it very easy for me, dear," he said piteously.

There came into her face, like an inspiration, a radiance of the tenderest fun. She put her hands one on each of his shoulders, and with a little soft catch in her voice, sang:—

> "Lady once loved a pig.
> 'Honey,' said she,
> 'Pig, will you marry me?'—

"*You* grunt!" she bade him.

He strove to turn his face away.

"Grunt," she besought. "Grunt, Pig; Perfect Pig! Grunt now or forever hold your peace."

Then the clinging hands slipped forward, the soft arms closed about his neck, and she was sobbing with her cheek pressed close to his cheek.

"I won't *let* you go. I won't! Never, never, never!"

"But I don't know what I'm to say to your father, darling," he said, as the grinding of the tender against the wharf brought them back to realities.

"Leave him to me," she bade him. "I'm going to send for him and Judge Enderby now."

The two appeared promptly.

"Dad," she said, "you remember what you said about the house on Battery Place?"

"I think I do."

"That you'd get it for me if you had to buy off the option for a million?"

"Correct."

"And you're still Wayne of his Word?"

"Try me."

"Give your check to Mr. Smith. Our price is just a million. Then," she added with an entrancing blush, "you can give us the house as a wedding present."

"So that's the bargain, is it?" queried the financier.

"No. It isn't the bargain at all," replied the Tyro, with quiet firmness. "The option isn't for sale."

"Not at a million?"

"Certainly not at a million. It isn't worth anything like that."

"A thing's worth what you can get for it."

"For value received. Not for charity, with however glossy a sugar-coating. If Miss Wayne—Cecily—"

"Little Miss Grouch," corrected the girl with the smile of a particularly pleased angel.

"If Little Miss Grouch marries me, she will have to marry me on what I'm honestly worth."

"I'm content," said Little Miss Grouch.

"So am I," said Mr. Wayne heartily. "You've come through, my boy." He set a friendly hand on the Tyro's shoulder. "As for Remsen Van Dam," he added, scratching his head ruefully, "I might have known that Cecily's pick would be better than mine. Look here, children," he added briskly, "let's get this thing over and done with away from the American papers. Enderby, how do Americans get married in England?"

"Give me five dol—I mean five hundred dollars," responded the Judge promptly.

"What for?"

"Advice."

"YOU'VE COME THROUGH, MY BOY"

"Done," said Mr. Wayne.

"And leave it to me. Let me see." He totaled up on his fingers. "Five and five is ten, and five is fifteen, and five hundred is five fifteen; a very fair profit on the voyage. It'll buy a wedding present for—"

"For the House of Smith on Battery Place," said Little Miss Grouch demurely.

THE END

THE CLARION
By Samuel Hopkins Adams

The story of an American city, the men who controlled it, the young editor who attempted to reform it, and the audacious girl who helped sway its destinies.

"A vivid and picturesque story." —*Boston Transcript.*

"One of the most important novels of the year—a vivid, strong, sincere story." —*New Orleans Times-Picayune.*

"A tremendously interesting novel—vivid and gripping." —*Chicago Tribune.*

"One of the most interestingly stirring stories of modern life yet published ... vividly told and of burning interest." —*Philadelphia Public Ledger.*

Illustrated. $1.35 *net.*

HOUGHTON MIFFLIN COMPANY   BOSTON AND NEW YORK

THE STREET OF SEVEN STARS
By Mary Roberts Rinehart

A story of two young lovers—students in far-away Vienna—and their struggle with poverty and temptation. Incidentally, a graphic picture of life in the war-worn city of the Hapsburgs.

From Letters to the Author:

"Fresh and clean and sweet—a story which makes one feel the better for having read it and wish that he could know all of your dear characters." —*California.*

"Little that has been written in the last decade has given me such pleasure, and nothing has moved me to pen to an author a word of praise until to-day." —*Utah.*

"'The Street of Seven Stars' will be read fifty years from now, and will still be helping people to be braver and better." —*New York.*

"It stands far above any recent fiction I have read." —*Massachusetts.*

"Quite the best thing you have ever written." —*Connecticut.*

$1.25 *net.*

HOUGHTON
MIFFLIN
COMPANY

BOSTON
AND
NEW YORK

THE POET
By Meredith Nicholson

A clever, kindly portrait of a famous living poet, interwoven with a charming love story.

"Not since Henry Harland told us the story of the gentle Cardinal and his snuffbox, have we had anything as idyllic as Meredith Nicholson's 'The Poet.'" — *New York Evening Sun.*

"This delightful story, so filled with blended poetry and common sense, reminds one, as he reaches instinctively for a parallel, of the rarely delicate and beautiful ones told by Thomas Bailey Aldrich." — *Washington Star.*

"A rare performance in American literature. Everybody knows who the Poet is, but if they want to know him as a kind of Good Samaritan in a different way than they know him in his verses, they should read this charming idyll." — *Boston Transcript.*

Illustrated in color. $1.30 *net.*

HOUGHTON MIFFLIN COMPANY   BOSTON AND NEW YORK

THE WITCH
By Mary Johnston

Miss Johnston's most successful historical novel, a romance glowing with imagination, adventure, and surging passions. The stormy days of Queen Elizabeth live again in this powerful tale of the "witch" and her lover.

"A well-told and effective story, the most artistic that Miss Johnston has written." —*New York Sun.*

"A powerful, realistic tale." —*New York World.*

"This is Mary Johnston's greatest book." —*Cleveland Plain Dealer.*

"An extraordinarily graphic picture of the witchcraft delusion in England in the age that followed Queen Elizabeth's death." —*San Francisco Chronicle.*

"Far more artistic than anything that Miss Johnston has written since 'To Have and To Hold.'" —*Providence Journal.*

With frontispiece in color. $1.40 *net.*

HOUGHTON
MIFFLIN
COMPANY

BOSTON
AND
NEW YORK

OVERLAND RED
By HARRY HERBERT KNIBBS

"Overland Red is a sort of mixture of Owen Wister's Virginian and David Harum." — *Chicago Evening Post.*

"Perfectly clean and decent and at the same time full of romantic adventure." — *Chicago Tribune.*

"A story tingling with the virile life of the great West in the days when a steady eye and a six-shooter were first aids to the law, 'Overland Red.' should be a widely read piece of fiction." — *Boston Globe.*

"A pulsing, blood-warming romance of California hills, mines, and ranges is 'Overland Red.' ... A book that should be sufficient to any author's pride." — *New York World.*

Illustrated in color. Crown 8vo, $1.35 *net.*

————————

HOUGHTON
MIFFLIN
COMPANY

BOSTON
AND
NEW YORK

————————

THE AFTER HOUSE
By MARY ROBERTS RINEHART

"An absorbing tale of murder and mystery—Mrs. Rinehart has written no more exciting story than this." — *New Orleans Picayune.*

"Succeeds to a remarkable degree in thrilling the reader ... she stands in direct line, and not unworthily, after Stevenson and that born teller of tales, F. Marion Crawford." —*Philadelphia Press.*

"Mrs. Rinehart has disclosed herself as an adept and ingenious inventor of thrilling murder puzzles, and in none of them has she told a story more directly and more fluently than in 'The After House.'" —*Boston Transcript.*

"Mrs. Rinehart has, with no small constructive skill, created a real mystery and left it unsolved until the very last.... Her incidents follow one another in rapid succession and the interest of the story is maintained to the very end. A good novel for quick reading." —*New York Herald.*

Illustrated by May Wilson Preston
12mo, $1.25 *net.*

HOUGHTON   BOSTON
MIFFLIN   AND
COMPANY   NEW YORK

THE SPARE ROOM
By Mrs. Romilly Fedden

"A bride and groom, a villa in Capri, a spare room and seven guests (assorted varieties) are the ingredients which go to make this thoroughly amusing book." —*Chicago Evening Post.*

"Bubbling over with laughter ... distinctly a book to read and chuckle over." —*Yorkshire Observer.*

"Mrs. Fedden has succeeded in arranging for her readers a constant fund of natural yet wildly amusing complications." —*Springfield Republican.*

"A clever bit of comedy that goes with spirit and sparkle, Mrs. Fedden's little story shows her to be a genuine humorist.... She deserves to be welcomed cordially to the ranks of those who can make us laugh." —*New York Times.*

"Brimful of rich humor." —*Grand Rapids Herald.*

Illustrated by Haydon Jones. 12mo.
$1.00 *net.*

HOUGHTON
MIFFLIN
COMPANY

BOSTON
AND
NEW YORK

V. V.'S EYES
By HENRY SYDNOR HARRISON

"'V. V.'s Eyes' is a novel of so elevated a spirit, yet of such strong interest, unartificial, and uncritical, that it is obviously a fulfillment of Mr. Harrison's intention to 'create real literature.'" —*Baltimore News.*

"In our judgment it is one of the strongest and at the same time most delicately wrought American novels of recent years." — *The Outlook.*

"'V. V.'s Eyes' is an almost perfect example of idealistic realism. It has the soft heart, the clear vision and the boundless faith in humanity that are typical of our American outlook on life." — *Chicago Record-Herald.*

"A delicate and artistic study of striking power and literary quality which may well remain the high-water mark in American fiction for the year.... Mr. Harrison definitely takes his place as the one among our younger American novelists of whom the most enduring work may be hoped for." — *Springfield Republican.*

Pictures by R. M. Crosby. Square crown 8vo. $1.35 *net.*

HOUGHTON   BOSTON
MIFFLIN   AND
COMPANY   NEW YORK

Lightning Source UK Ltd.
Milton Keynes UK
UKHW010703040521
383104UK00003B/281